Enid Blyton

THE SECRET SEVEN

Look Out, Secret Seven

ILLUSTRATED BY *Tony Ross*

h

Hodder
Children's
Books

A division of Hachette Children's Books

Text copyright © Hodder & Stoughton Ltd
Illustrations copyright © Tony Ross

First published in Great Britain in 1962 by Hodder & Stoughton Ltd
This edition published in 2013

The rights of Enid Blyton and Tony Ross to be identified as the Author
and Illustrator of the Work respectively have been asserted by them in
accordance with the Copyright, Designs and Patents Act 1988

1

A Catalogue record for this book is available from the British Library

ISBN 978 1 44491356 9

Typeset by Hewer Text UK Ltd, Edinburgh
Printed and bound in Great Britain by Clays Ltd, St Ives plc

The paper and board used in this paperback by Hodder Children's Books are natural
recyclable products made from wood grown in sustainable forests. The manufacturing
processes conform to the environmental regulations of the country of origin.

Hodder Children's Books
a division of Hachette Children's Books
338 Euston Road, London NW1 3BH
An Hachette UK company

www.hodderchildrens.co.uk

Enid Blyton®

THE SECRET SEVEN

Look Out, Secret Seven

Have you read them all?

CONTENTS

CHAPTER ONE

HOLIDAYS AT LAST

'HOLIDAYS AT *last*!' said Peter, coming in at the back door, and flinging his school satchel right across the kitchen. It struck the chair that the cat was lying in, and she gave a yowl of fright and disappeared at top speed through the open window.

'Now what did you want to frighten old Puss for?' demanded Rachel, the housekeeper, rolling out pastry fiercely. 'Sleeping there peacefully after catching mice all night in your father's barn!'

'I didn't know she was there,' said Peter. 'Honestly I didn't. May I have a dig into that jampot, Rachel?'

'You may not,' said Rachel. 'Where's your sister? Oh my, oh my – holidays again, and you two poking round my kitchen all the time. What a life!'

'Rachel, you'll have *two* people to run your errands, and scrape out dishes, and tell you that your apple-pie is the best in the world,' said Peter. 'And . . .'

'Yes – and two people taking buns out of my tin, and wanting raisins to eat at all times, and asking for home-made lemonade, and . . .'

Janet, Peter's sister, came running in, flung her arms round Rachel and gave her a smacking kiss.

'What's for dinner?' she said.

'You two don't think of anything but food,' grumbled Rachel, giving her pastry a good roll. 'You'd better go into the sitting-room to your mother. Your godmother's with her – and if I know anything about her, she'll have brought you a present – sweets or something.'

Peter and Janet went at once to the sitting-room. They were very fond of their godmother, Auntie Lou. They each gave her a hug, and informed her that the holidays had now begun.

'So we can come over and see you, if you like,' said Peter.

'Wait till you are asked, Peter,' said his mother. 'And what *have* you been doing to your knees? I cannot *think* how you get them so black. Anyone would suppose you walked back from school on them over all the mud you could find.'

'I'll go and wash them,' said Peter, looking down at them in horror. 'Mother, I honestly *don't* know how they—'

'Well, just let me give you my little holiday present,' said his godmother. 'I can't wait while you wash your knees, I have to catch the bus. I imagine you still like chocolate?'

And she handed over to him a large tin box, so large that Peter and Janet couldn't believe it contained just chocolates. 'I know you have a club of some sort,' she said. 'Seven or eight of you, aren't there? Well, I thought you'd like this tin of chocolate biscuits for your next meeting.'

Peter took off the lid – and stared in delight.

'Janet, look – dozens and dozens of chocolate biscuits of all kinds! Gosh! Mother, I shall call a meeting at once. Oh, Auntie Lou, you *are* generous! Are they really all for us?'

'For you and your friends,' said his godmother, getting up. 'Now I really must catch my bus. Come and see me off.'

So off they all went to see Auntie Lou safely into the bus. Then back to the sitting-room – and the tin of biscuits.

'Let's not eat a single one ourselves till we call a meeting of the Secret Seven,' said Peter. 'We'll offer them to Mother and Rachel, but we won't take *any* ourselves. It's ages since we had a good meeting – and these will make a meeting go like anything.'

'We'll call one tomorrow,' said Janet, happily. 'Oh, to think it's holidays again – with meetings down in the shed – and passwords and badges, and . . .'

'Passwords – *pass*words – now what in the world was our last one?' said Peter.

'That's easy,' said Janet. 'We chose "Holidays" because we knew the hols would be here when we had the next meeting. I bet everyone remembers it. Let's go round to all the members tonight – or telephone – and tell them there's a meeting tomorrow – at, say, five o'clock.'

'But that's tea-time,' said Peter.

'Of course, silly – and those chocolate biscuits will be just right for then,' said Janet.

'Yes – they will,' said Peter. 'Couldn't you write notes to tell the others of the meeting, Janet? It's – well, it's a bit more official.'

'You write them then,' said Janet. 'You're more official than I am. You're the head of the club.'

'Well – perhaps it would be *quicker* to telephone,' said Peter. 'Ha – it will be great to have the Secret Seven going again. I do hope something exciting turns up.'

'It usually does,' said Janet. 'Especially if that awful Susie is about.'

'Jack says Susie's been worse than ever lately,' said Peter. 'If *I* had a sister like Susie I'd sit on her all the time, and . . .'

'Then you'd have a mighty uncomfortable seat!' said Janet. 'Nobody's ever got the better of Susie yet. I bet she'll come to the meeting tomorrow, if she can.'

'Well, she won't get in, if she does come,' said Peter. 'Ah, Scamper – there you are. WHY weren't you here to welcome us back for the holidays?'

Scamper was their lovely golden spaniel. He had been with Matt the shepherd up on the hills, playing with Shadow, Matt's faithful old sheep-dog. Then he had suddenly remembered that Peter had told him the holidays began today. HOLIDAYS! Scamper knew that word well – it meant days and days of Peter's and Janet's company, it meant walks, and games, and titbits of all kinds.

So Scamper had given Shadow a sudden apologetic bark, and, to the collie's surprise, had raced down the hill as fast as a hare, his long ears flapping up and down. HOLIDAYS!

Soon he was barking in delight round the two

children – and then he suddenly sniffed chocolate. Ha, chocolate biscuits – better still!

'You shall have the very first one,' said Janet, taking a biscuit from the top layer. 'Catch!'

Snap! It was in Scamper's mouth – one crunch, and it was gone!

'Biscuits are really *wasted* on you, Scamper,' said Janet. 'I don't believe you even *taste* them. We're calling a meeting of the Secret Seven tomorrow – you'd like to come, wouldn't you?'

'WOOF!' said Scamper, joyfully, his stump of a tail wagging like clockwork. Meetings! Biscuits! Holidays! Woof, woof – life was going to be FUN!

CHAPTER TWO

A SHOCK FOR THE SECRET SEVEN

IN THE evening Peter and Janet telephoned to the other members of the Secret Seven, and told them about the meeting, and the enormous tin of chocolate biscuits.

'If you'd like to bring something to drink – orange-ade or lemonade, for instance – we'll provide the mugs,' said Peter.

Soon all the members knew of the meeting and Peter put down the telephone for the last time. 'Phew – I do hate telephoning,' he said. 'Everyone wants to be so *chatty*!'

'Well, you sounded pretty chatty yourself when you spoke to George and Colin,' said Janet. 'And what a pity Susie came to the telephone when you wanted to speak to Jack! Now she knows there's a meeting she'll try and play one of her usual silly tricks – I bet she won't give Jack your message.'

'She said she was going to a fancy-dress party tomorrow,' said Peter. 'So we'll be safe from her for once.'

'Oh yes – I remember now,' said Janet. 'Her cousin's giving a fancy-dress affair tomorrow afternoon. I wonder what Susie's going as. That awful friend of hers, Binkie, is going too.'

'Susie said they were going as Jack and Jill,' said Peter. 'But I bet they won't bother to take a pail of water with them. *I'd* like to empty a pail of very, very cold water over Susie's head.'

'You'd never get the chance,' said Janet, with a giggle at the thought of Peter throwing water over that monkey of a Susie. '*She'd* souse *you* before you could stop her.'

'Don't be silly,' said Peter. 'I'd never let her do a thing like that. Now listen – we'll have to be pretty busy tomorrow if we're going to meet in the shed. You'll have to find those green letters, S.S., and pin them on to the door – we took them off because they were getting wet with all that rain, you remember. And for goodness' sake find our badges.'

'I put them away safely in my jewel-case,' said Janet. 'So you needn't worry.'

'Well, I hope you'll find them there,' said Peter. '*Last* time I saw your jewel-case it had sweets in it, and a new rubber, and a bit of sealing-wax, a broken brooch, a—'

'You'd no right to look into my jewel-case,' said Janet, 'and I shall—'

'All right, all right,' said Peter, hastily. 'Let's not quarrel when there's so much to do. I hope the gardener hasn't taken away the boxes we used to sit on in the shed. And Scamper, I hope you've been keeping down the mice and rats there for us. I should feel very ashamed of you tomorrow evening if a few rats came to join us.'

'Ugh! What a horrible thought!' said Janet. Scamper gave a loud bark at the same time, as if to tell her that all the rats and mice had been safely dealt with. He decided to go down to the shed the first thing next morning to make quite sure there wasn't even a sniff of them.

It was very pleasant next day to turn out the old shed and make it tidy and clean. The gardener popped his head in at the door, grunted and went away again, nodding his head in approval of all the tidying up going on.

"Bout time too,' they heard him mutter as he went up the path. Janet looked round the clean shed, pleased with their work. Boxes to sit on – mugs on the little shelf, ready for any drinks that were brought – seven little plastic plates for the biscuits, one for each member – the tin itself standing proudly on a little box of its own – and an old, rather raggedy rug on the earth floor.

'Nice!' said Janet. 'The shed smells a bit of apples, doesn't it, Peter – there were some stored here in the winter, you know. I've put the S.S. on the door. It's a pity the shed has such a small window, it makes it rather dark in here. But it's not dark enough for candles, is it?'

'No,' said Peter. 'Anyway, Mother gets scared if we have candles down here – says Scamper is sure to knock one over and then up would go the shed in flames, and . . .'

'And the fire-engine would come, and we'd have the most exciting meeting we've ever had,' said Janet.

The meeting was to begin at five o'clock, and at five to five Peter, Janet, and Scamper were sitting in the shed, waiting. Scamper eyed the tin of biscuits longingly, and gave pathetic little whines, as if to say he was so hungry that he couldn't wait another second for a meal.

Then he suddenly whined excitedly. He had heard footsteps! 'The others are coming,' said Peter, pleased. 'Nice and punctual, too.'

Bang-bang. That was someone knocking on the shed door.

'Password, please!' called Peter, and Pam's and Barbara's voices answered at once.

'Holidays!'

Peter opened the door, grinning. 'Right!' he said. 'Come in. Hallo, here comes someone else. Password, please!'

'Holidays!' said Colin's voice. No sooner was he in the shed than there came another knock – this time it was George.

'Password!' shouted Peter.

'Peter, is it "Holidays"?' asked George. 'Thank goodness it is! Hey, isn't it nice to be the Secret Seven again? Are we all here? It's a bit dark in the shed this evening.'

'Only Jack to come,' said Peter. 'I think I can hear him now. Yes, here he is. Password, Jack!'

'Holidays', came the answer, and then the door was shut on the Seven. The meeting was about to begin!

And then, very surprisingly, Scamper suddenly began to growl! He sat in a dark corner of the shed and growled and growled without stopping. Everyone stared at him in wonder.

'What's up, Scamper?' asked Peter, but the only answer was another fierce growl. It really was very puzzling.

'Scamper seems to be growling at JACK!' said Pam. 'Look at him staring at him. He's even showing his teeth!'

'He's never done that before to any of us,' said Janet. 'Stop it, Scamper. Jack, take off your cap, perhaps that's why Scamper's growling. You forgot to take it off when you came in.'

'Er – I think I'd better keep it on,' said Jack. 'I've – er – a bit of a cold in my head.'

George suddenly whipped off the cap – and everyone stared in amazement and anger. Hair tumbled out from under the cap – but not short hair!

'It's SUSIE! Susie, not Jack! Susie, how DARE you dress up in Jack's clothes and come to a meeting?' shouted Peter.

'Well – Binkie and I were on our way home from a fancy-dress party, and we thought we'd look in on our way past,' grinned Susie. 'We went as Jack and Jill, you see. I'm Jack – and Binkie, who's hiding outside, is Jill. Jack lent me his clothes, so that I could be a boy at the party – and my voice and his are alike, so it was easy to get into your meeting. Ha ha – I heard your password being said – you really are a lot of simpletons, you know – and here I am!'

'And Scamper was the only sensible one among us!' groaned George. '*He* knew it wasn't old Jack sitting here with us! Get out, Susie. GET OUT!'

'With pleasure,' said Susie, and stood up, still with a most infuriating grin on her face. 'Jack will be along here soon. I told him the meeting was at half-past five, instead of five, so it's not his fault he's late. Am I clever enough to be one of the Secret Seven?'

But that was too much for Peter. He gave Susie a push to send her out of the shed, but she wouldn't go, and, instead, began to yell.

'Binkie! Help, Binkie!'

She rushed out of the shed door with all the others following her in a real rage – and then, quite suddenly, something very cold and wet descended on them, soaking their heads and shoulders!

'Oh – sorry – that was the pail of water we took as Jack and Jill!' called Susie, with a squeal of laughter. 'Good shot, Binkie! Good night, all – hope you have a very pleasant meeting!'

And off went the two wicked girls, very pleased indeed with their evening's work. To be One Up on the Secret Seven was wonderful. Oh what a tale to tell their giggling friends!

CHAPTER THREE

A VERY GOOD MEETING

THE SIX left in the shed were too angry for words. Peter shook his fist after the two running girls, and yelled in fury.

'We're soaked! HOW DARE YOU! You wait till we see you again!'

But all the answer they had was the sound of running feet – and distant squeals of laughter. That Susie! How could she even have THOUGHT of such a trick? Poor Jack – fancy having a sister like that!

'Borrowing his clothes too, to be Jack in the nursery rhyme,' groaned Peter, mopping his shoulder with an old sack, 'AND having a pail of water too! I'm wet through!'

'And fancy telling Jack the meeting wasn't till half-past five – no wonder he's late!' said Janet. 'I'll fetch an old towel from the house, Peter. You're the wettest because you were nearest.'

'No, don't. You'll only have Mother asking what's happened. Oh, that awful Susie! I'll tell Jack exactly what I think of her when he comes!'

But Jack didn't come. Poor Jack! He was just about to start off when Susie and Binkie came rolling with laughter up the drive, the pail clanking between them. When they told him what had happened, he sat down on the front steps and groaned.

'SUSIE! HOW COULD you go to the meeting and pretend to be me? HOW COULD you tell me the wrong time? I can't possibly go to the meeting. I'll have to telephone and apologise for your behaviour – and probably I'll be chucked out of the club!'

'*We* don't mind writing and apologising,' said Susie. 'I don't mind writing a *dozen* apologies – it was *worth* a dozen to crash in on the meeting, and bamboozle everyone – and Binkie was SUCH a good shot with the water!'

'Didn't *anyone* spot that you weren't me?' said Jack in wonder.

'Only Scamper. He growled like anything,' said Susie. 'Oh, I'm going to start laughing again – oh Binkie, did you think our pail of water would be so *useful?*'

Jack went off in disgust and disappointment. He had been looking forward to the meeting so much. Now he couldn't possibly go. He went to the telephone to apologise for Susie's behaviour – but just as he was about to lift the receiver, the bell rang. It was Janet on the phone.

'Jack? Jack, it really *is* you, not Susie, isn't it?' said Janet's anxious voice. 'This is just to say that the meeting is off for tonight – we're all rather wet! I expect Susie has told you all about it. No, don't apologise for her, Jack – *you* weren't to blame. But Peter wants me to say the meeting is postponed till tomorrow. Will you come then?'

'Yes. Yes, I'd love to,' said Jack, much relieved. 'Thanks awfully. Actually I was just coming along now, so I'm glad you rang. No – no, of course I won't tell Susie about the next meeting. But why don't you go on with tonight's?'

'We're too wet and cross,' said Janet. 'We'll see you tomorrow, then. Goodbye!'

So, the next night, the Secret Seven met once more, and this time there was no growling from Scamper, for it really was Jack there, not Susie! Everyone made quite a fuss of Jack, for he felt so ashamed and forlorn to think that his sister had spoilt a meeting.

'Cheer up, Jack – it had its funny side,' said Pam, kindly.

'*Had* it? Well, I can't say *I* noticed it,' said Peter. 'However, let's get on with this meeting. Scamper, please keep your ears cocked for any sound outside.'

Scamper at once went to the door, and put his head on one side. Now no one could even *creep* near! Scamper could hear the smallest sound – even the feet of a night-beetle running by on the path outside!

The meeting went quite well. The tin of chocolate biscuits was a great success. There were so many biscuits in it that everyone was able to have at least six – and Scamper had a generous share! He ate his biscuits over by the door, determined not to let anyone come in unless he recognised voice and footsteps!

'Now,' said Peter, when biscuits had been eaten and orangeade and lemonade drunk, 'now – if this club is going to continue properly, we'll have to decide on doing something together.'

'Like helping somebody?' asked Pam. 'Mother says we ought to help some charity if we can't think of anything to do. She says it's silly to have a club that just meets and eats and talks.'

'Well, I like *that*! We've done heaps of things in this club!' said Janet, indignantly. 'Helped people – solved mysteries – and the very last thing we did was to find that dog-stealer. The one who stole the shepherd's sheep-dog, Shadow – and stole Scamper as well, and—'

'All right, all right,' said Pam. 'I know all that. I'm only telling you what my mother says.'

'Well, it's fun to have some *aim*, some *interest*,' said Barbara. 'You know – something to think about and puzzle about. Just think of the exciting things that have happened to us – and now here we sit, just eating more and more biscuits, the same as last time. We don't seem to have a brain between us.'

Peter listened, and frowned. 'You know – Barbara's right,' he said. 'We MUST think of something to do. We've plenty of brains between us – we know that. Now – who has any ideas? Speak up, please.'

There was a very long, frowning silence. 'I never *can* think of any good ideas when I'm ordered to,' complained Janet. 'The best ideas aren't ones I think out – they're the ones that come in a flash!'

'Isn't there some mystery we can try to solve?' asked George. 'Or someone we can help in some way?'

'Well – there's only *one* mystery I know about – and that's to find out who tied our headmaster's chair

23

half-way up the flag-pole in the school grounds,' said Colin, with a spurt of laughter. 'You can't think how daft it looked there last Wednesday, when we went to school.'

'It would be a waste of time to solve such a silly little mystery,' said Pam. 'In fact, I wouldn't be a bit surprised if it didn't turn out to be that awful Susie who managed to put it there – with her friend Binkie's help!'

That made everyone laugh, even Jack. There was a short silence, and then Colin spoke up.

'Er – I've just thought of an idea – *not* a very good one, I'm afraid. What about trying to get old General Branksome's medals back for him? They've been stolen, you know.'

Everyone stared at Colin in surprise. 'But how on earth could we do that?' asked George. 'Even the police don't know who took them or where they are.'

'The old man lives next door to me,' said Colin. 'And – well – he's very old, you know, and his medals meant a lot to him. And – er – yesterday I saw him telling somebody about them, in his garden – it's next to ours – and it was awful, because tears ran down his cheeks all the time.'

There was a shocked silence. Grown-ups hardly ever cried; and soldiers *never*. And yet the old General had had tears running down his cheeks. How unhappy he must be!

Nobody knew quite what to say. The silence went on, broken by a mournful whine from Scamper, who couldn't imagine why everyone was suddenly so quiet.

'It's all right, Scamper. We're just considering something important,' said Janet, stroking his silky head. 'We're talking about crying, and that's something dogs don't understand. Animals can't cry.'

Scamper whimpered again, as if he quite disagreed with what Janet said. Then George asked a question.

'Can't the General have his medals replaced by the Government?'

'Of course not,' said Colin. 'Anyway, some of them were medals awarded to him by foreign countries. He was a very, very brave man, you know. I simply couldn't *bear* to see him crying like that. I suppose the thief stole not only the medals, but all his memories – if you know what I mean. Anyway, that's what my father said, and he has one or two medals of his own, so he ought to know what he's talking about. *He* was brave too, in the last war. I *wish* we could get back the General's medals!'

Pam and the other two girls were very much touched by Colin's suggestion. None of them could bear to think of so old and so very brave a man weeping for his lost medals.

'I vote we try to find the medals,' said Pam. 'I don't know how we're going to set about it, but I vote we try.'

'Well – *I* think it's rather an impossible task,' said Peter. 'I do really. *I* vote that we set ourselves some other job as well. Surely the Secret Seven can tackle *two* things!'

'What's the second task to be, then?' asked Jack.

'I vote we keep an eye on nesting birds in Bramley Woods,' said Peter. 'There's apparently a gang going about there, pulling nests to pieces, and killing the young birds – and taking any eggs as well. Well – there are seven of us – what about doing something about it? Scamper would help too!'

'WUFF!' said Scamper, at the top of his voice. So it was settled. The Secret Seven had two tasks – one to look into the matter of the missing medals – and two, to watch for nest-destroyers in Bramley Woods.

'It's a funny mixture, really,' said George, rather doubtfully. 'They don't exactly go together, those two things, do they?'

'Not really,' said Janet. 'But you never know, George, you never know!'

CHAPTER FOUR

COLIN DOES HIS BIT

THERE WAS no time to make any further plans, because there came a sudden clanging of a bell from Peter's house away up the garden.

'Goodness – that's Mother ringing our bell,' said Peter, looking at his watch. 'We must go, Janet. Gosh, I didn't know it was so late. That's the worst of our meetings – the time simply *flies* by!'

'Yes, but wait a minute, Peter,' said George. 'What exactly do we do next? Hadn't someone better go to see the General, and find out a little about the medals – when they were stolen, and how, and all that?'

'Yes. Yes, of course,' said Peter. 'Well, I think Colin should do that as he lives next door to the General, and knows him. Will you, Colin?'

28

'Er – yes. I suppose it had better be me,' said Colin, frowning. 'Gosh, I hope he won't mind my asking him questions. He might think me rather inquisitive.'

'Well, after all, he does *know* you,' said Pam. 'You can be very sympathetic, you know – you're good at that – and anyway you *are* very sorry for him. He might not like *strangers* probing into the disappearance of his precious medals, but surely he wouldn't mind *you* being interested.'

'And as for the other thing the Secret Seven mean to do, we'd better arrange with one another to go walking through the woods and look out for anyone disturbing or destroying nests,' said Peter. 'I suggest you all wear your badges when you go – then you can say that you are under orders from your club to protect birds' nests.'

'Do we take people's names, or what?' asked Barbara, looking rather scared.

'Well – you can *ask* for names and addresses,' said Peter. 'You probably won't get them, but it'll upset silly kids if they think people are on the watch for nest-destroyers. After all, there's been a lot about this in the papers, you know, and children *have* been asked to do everything they can to try to stop any cruelty.'

'We'll go about in twos or threes,' said Jack. 'We'll feel braver then!'

'Right,' said Peter. 'Well, make your own plans please, team up with each other, and do what you can. Report back at the club in four days' time – and if you want to call a meeting before then, for any reason, leave a note down in the shed. Janet or I will see it, for we come down each day.'

'Right,' said Jack. 'Hey, there's your bell ringing again, Peter. You'll get into trouble, you and Janet.'

They all said goodbye. Peter and Janet shut the shed door, and, with Scamper at their heels, raced up to the house.

'*Just* in time!' said Rachel, who was standing with the bell at the kitchen door. 'I've taken in supper, but your father's still washing his hands. Hurry up now, or you'll get into trouble.'

The other members of the club made their ways home. Colin thought deeply as he walked down his road. He dreaded the task of talking to the old General. Suppose the old man thought him inquisitive or impertinent, and shouted at him as Colin had heard him shouting at an impudent tradesman? Suppose he complained to Colin's parents?

Oh well, thought Colin, I've been given this job to do by the Secret Seven. And after all, *I* put up the idea. But, oh dear – how in the world am I to set about it?

Colin thought about it in bed that night. He decided that the next morning, when the General took his walk down the garden and back, he would throw his ball over the wall. Then I'll sit on the wall, and apologise, and ask if I can slip down into his garden and find my ball, thought Colin. And maybe we'll get into conversation, and I can ask him a few questions. Yes – that's what I'll do.

So, next morning, Colin took his ball and sat at his bedroom window, watching for the General to take his walk down the garden. Ah – there he was!

Colin ran downstairs and through the kitchen into the garden. He carefully threw his ball over the wall, aiming at some thick bushes well away from the old General. Then he shinned up on to the wall-top, and called cheerfully to the old man.

'Good morning.'

'Oh – good morning, Colin,' said the General, blinking up at him. 'Not at school?'

'No. It's holidays now,' said Colin. 'Look, I'm so sorry, but I'm afraid my ball flew into your garden. May I get it? I promise not to tread on the beds.'

'Yes, yes, of course, my boy,' said General Branksome, leaning on his stick. 'I never mind good-mannered boys coming into my garden. Come along down. And what about a glass of lemonade with me?'

Colin was delighted. That meant a nice little talk! He leapt down, found his ball, and rejoined the General, who was now walking back to the house. The old man shouted for his cook in a loud voice.

'Emma! EMMA! I have company. Two lemonades please, and some biscuits. EMMA!'

Emma duly appeared, smiling at Colin, and soon he and the old man were sitting together in the tiny little sitting-room, whose walls were covered with photographs of the General and his soldier friends, and of exciting pictures of old battles. But one space, over the mantelpiece, was bare.

Colin knew why. That was where the General had displayed his medals, glittering there in their velvet-lined case, set with coloured ribbons. The General saw him looking at the bare space, and sighed heavily. The old man began to talk to Colin in his slow voice.

'I expect you heard about someone stealing my medals. To think of a cowardly *thief* owning them! Boy, those medals were won by bravery and daring, by wounds and pain. They were all I had left to show that I was once a fine soldier. I'm an old man now, and nobody thinks much of me – but once people see those medals, ha – they change their minds. They look at me with different eyes. They don't see the poor lame old fellow I am now – they see someone who had DONE things! And now my medals are gone, and I feel old, old, old! I could still feel young when I had them to look at . . .'

To Colin's intense dismay the old man burst into tears, and the boy wished he had never thrown his ball over the wall. He had no right to stir up the old man's grief.

'I'll *find* them for you!' Colin heard himself saying, touching the old man's coat-sleeve. 'I'll find them, I promise you. Don't you fret, you shall have them back. LISTEN TO ME. I'LL FIND THEM!'

The old General was as astonished to hear Colin saying this, as Colin himself was. He shook the boy by the hand with an astonishingly firm grip.

'I believe you, boy! I *believe* you'll find them! Ah, you're a boy after my own heart! You'll be winning medals yourself some day, you will! Ah, here's Emma. Emma, what do you want? Can't you see I've a visitor?'

'Yes. And I can see you've been upsetting yourself about them medals again,' said Emma, patting the old man's back. 'Now, you let the boy go back home, and you have a nice sleep. You didn't have a good night, you know, worrying yourself. You just have a nice lie-down.'

Colin felt in the way. He slid off through the door, and found himself in the kitchen. He stood waiting for Emma to come back. She came in, shaking her head.

'There now – he's having a rest. You shouldn't have talked about the medals. He thinks of them night and day.'

'Do the police know who stole them yet?' asked Colin.

'No. All we know is that somebody got in one night and took the lot – left no finger-prints either. But we do know that he – or she maybe – must have had a mighty small hand, for he had to put his fist carefully through that little hole there – in that broken pane, see – in order to undo the catch and open the window from the inside. I doubt if *you* could put your hand through that broken pane.'

'I'll try,' said Colin. But no, he couldn't wriggle it through the sharp hole without cutting his hand. 'I should have thought that only a small child could get his or her hand through, and reach up to that catch,' he said, puzzled. 'But surely a child wouldn't think of stealing a soldier's *medals*!'

'It's a mystery,' said Emma. 'The poor old gentleman was almost off his head with shock. He's offering a good reward, you know – five hundred pounds!

Maybe someone will find the medals hidden away somewhere, and claim the reward.'

'Five hundred pounds!' said Colin, amazed. 'Good gracious – what a lot of money! I wish *I* could find them. But I wouldn't take the reward from the old General.'

'You're a nice boy,' said Emma, approvingly. 'You come and look in my larder and see if there's anything you fancy. I've some fine home-made meringues there!'

'Oh no, thank you very much,' said Colin. But kind old Emma forced two large meringues on him – and they were very, VERY good!

Well – he certainly had something to report at the next meeting. But it didn't really look as if he had any *real* clues to the mystery, except that it was probably someone with a very small hand who had forced that window. And Colin was quite certain that every Suspect that came along would have extremely *large* hands! Things always went contrariwise when you were trying to puzzle out something. Colin went red as he remembered how he had promised the General that he would get back his medals for him – whatever had made him say such a thing! He must have been mad! The Secret Seven would be sure to disapprove of such silly talk – and quite right too.

What's the time? he thought, and looked at his watch. Quite early still. I think I'll hare off to Bramley Woods and join the others there – if only I can find them. I really *must* tell them what's happened. We'll *have* to get back those medals *some*how!

He ran next door to his own home and popped into the kitchen. His mother was there, very busy.

'Mother – *could* I make myself some sandwiches and go off to Bramley Woods to join Jack and the others?' he begged.

'Well, look – there are some rolls over from breakfast. Butter those, and take some tomatoes,' said his mother. 'Spread the rolls with shrimp paste if you like. And there are plenty of macaroons in the tin, and you can have some biscuits, and . . .'

'Oooh, *thanks*, Mother – wonderful!' said Colin, gratefully. In five minutes he had his lunch in a plastic bag and was off and away. Now to find the others!

CHAPTER FIVE

BIRD-NESTERS - AND A RESCUE

AT THE same time that Colin was talking to the old
General, three others of the Secret Seven were on
their way to Bramley Woods. They were Jack,
Barbara and George. They had decided to picnic
there, and, at the same time, keep a watch on
would-be-egg-hunters.

'We'll be doing our duty and having fun as well,'
said Jack.

'I rather hope we *don't* spot anyone looking for
nests,' said Barbara. 'I honestly should be scared to
go up and tackle them.'

'We boys will do that,' said George. 'You can just
stand by and agree with everything we say. Listen –
there's the cuckoo!'

'Perhaps we ought to go and find *him* and tick him off!' said Barbara.

'What on earth for?' asked Jack, astonished.

'Well, you know jolly well that cuckoos go to other birds' nests and throw out their eggs to smash on the ground,' said Barbara. 'Then the hen cuckoo quietly lays her own there instead – and the bird who owns the nest sits on the cuckoo's egg and hatches it out, never thinking that it isn't one of her own.'

'Well – I never knew *that*!' said Jack. 'How in the world did the cuckoo think of such a labour-saving idea?'

'Cuckoo!' called the distant bird. 'Cuckoo! Cuckoo!'

'You can play hide-and-seek by yourself!' shouted Jack. 'And if I find one of your eggs in another bird's nest, I shall take it out!'

'Cuckoo!' shouted the bird, almost as if it were calling Jack names. 'Cuckoo!'

There seemed to be no one about in the woods that morning. Barbara felt rather relieved. It really was too lovely a morning to pick a quarrel with anyone about bird-nesting. They wandered about among the trees, and Barbara picked a great bunch of primroses.

'Well, even if we're not doing a job for the Secret Seven, we're having a nice time,' said Barbara. 'What about sitting down and having an apple each? The birds are singing so madly I'd like to keep quiet and listen to them.'

As they were sitting on the primrosy ground, they heard voices not far off, and soon a little group of three came into sight – all boys about Jack's age. They wandered along, and then Jack and the others saw one boy pointing up into a tree.

'Bother – he's probably found a nest,' said George. Sure enough the boy began to scramble up the tree, and soon he yelled down.

'Blackbird's nest – four lovely eggs in it! Shall I take them all?'

'Take three – one for each of us!' shouted back another boy.

'This is where we butt in,' said Jack, getting to his feet. 'Come on.'

They all went over to the tree, and Jack spoke firmly, but politely.

'I expect you know we've all been asked not to rob birds' nests this spring – there was so much of it last year that the birds have been deserting this neighbourhood and they—'

'Listen to him!' said one boy, with a loud laugh. 'Little preacher, isn't he? Give him an egg, Larry!'

The boy up the tree took an egg from the blackbird's nest and threw it straight at poor Jack. It broke and ran down his face.

'I'll pull you down, I'll pull you down!' yelled Jack, in a rage, wiping the yellow yolk off his cheek, and trying to grab the boy's foot at the same time. But that was no good at all. The other boy barged into Jack and down they went, landing in the middle of a thick bush. A bird immediately flew out in fright.

'Ha – there must be a nest there too,' said the third boy. 'Let's look!'

Barbara suddenly felt desperate. She simply could *not* stand by and see a second bird's nest robbed and probably destroyed. She called out in a rather trembly voice:

'We belong to a club that has been given instructions to stop this sort of thing. I shall report you! Look – we're wearing badges. You clear off at once!'

The boy up the tree, and the boys below, stared at Barbara in surprise. Then they laughed. 'Look at her silly little badge – it's got S.S. on. I suppose the letters stand for Silly Snoopers! Ha – Silly Snoopers – just about right! Give me your badge – I'll put it into a bird's nest and see what it hatches into!'

He snatched at Barbara's badge, but Jack at once stepped in front. The boy lunged out and Jack suddenly found himself lying on his back in the grass. Barbara gave a scream. The boy up the tree dropped down on top of poor George, and he too found himself on the ground.

'Run, Barbara, run!' yelled Jack, sure that the boys would attack Barbara next. She ran in fright, calling for help, and to her great relief she saw a man lying down reading, under a tree. He leapt to his feet when he saw the running girl.

'What's the matter?' he shouted, and Barbara stopped at once.

'Oh will you come and help? We tried to stop some boys who were taking birds' eggs, and they've got my two friends down and . . .'

'Right,' said the man, and raced off in the direction of loud shouts coming from Jack and George. Both boys were most relieved to see a grown-up suddenly arriving.

The man yelled at the two boys who were now sitting firmly on top of Jack and George. 'Get up! You know bird-nesting is strictly forbidden in this wood. I'll take all your names. Here, you – what's *your* name?'

He caught hold of one of the boys sitting on top of Jack, and yanked him to his feet. But now the three bird-nesters were terrified, and with one accord they ran off at top speed, leaving Jack and George to scramble to their feet.

'Hey – thanks!' said Jack, gratefully. 'Thanks awfully. We were just trying to stop those wretched boys from robbing nests.'

'Are you a club of nature-lovers?' asked the man, seeing the S.S. badges that the three children were wearing.

'Well – we *are* nature-lovers – but our badges mean that we all belong to the Secret Seven Club,' said George. 'And one of the things we've been told to do is to prevent nest-robbing.'

'And a very good thing too,' said the man. 'I'm like you – I love birds and their nests. My word, there are a lot in this wood. I've found about forty already.'

'But you don't take their eggs, do you?' said Barbara.

'Good gracious no!' said the man. 'Actually I mean to write a book about the nests I have found during the last few years.'

'Er – would you care to share a picnic with us?' asked Jack, thinking that this man might be very interesting. 'We've brought food and drink with us, and we've plenty to spare.'

'Well, that's *very* kind of you,' said the man. He felt in his pocket, and pulled out a large paper packet. 'I've brought sandwiches, too. You have some of mine and I'll have some of yours. Let's sit down over there, on that nice mossy spot – and you can tell me about your club!'

So down they all sat on soft moss, and opened their packages. It wasn't *really* time to have their picnic – but somehow they all felt suddenly hungry.

'This is fun!' said Barbara, and the other three nodded as they munched ham sandwiches, and drank lemonade from small bottles.

'Good thing you were near,' said George, to the man who had come to their help. 'A *very* good thing!

Why, those three might have taken our badges away. Would you like to hear about our club? Right – I'll tell you!'

And there goes George, explaining all about the Secret Seven. How proud he is – and how well the stranger listens!

CHAPTER SIX

TOM SMITH IS RATHER SURPRISING

'WELL, I must say that I like the sound of your club,' said the man. 'Good badges too – did you make them yourselves?'

'The girls made them,' said George. 'We all meet in a shed with S.S. on the door – and we have great fun.'

'We sometimes help people who are in trouble,' said Barbara, 'and we sometimes solve mysteries, and . . .'

'Good gracious! And what mystery are you solving at the moment?' asked the man. 'By the way, my name is Smith – Tom Smith. Call me Tom, if you like.'

'Well – we'll call you Tom, if you really don't mind,' said Jack.

'Right,' said Tom Smith. 'Now – is the club doing anything besides stopping bird-nesters? Any great mystery being solved, or . . .'

'Well, one of the Secret Seven – Colin – is trying to solve a mystery about a robbery,' said Jack, importantly. 'We gave him that job because he happens to live next door to the man who was robbed.'

'This is all very interesting,' said Tom Smith, taking a currant bun. 'Who's the man who was robbed – and does he know you're helping him?'

'Well – he probably knows by now,' said Jack. 'Colin had to start on the job while we came here to do our bit in preventing bird-nesters taking eggs. I don't suppose you've heard of General Branksome, have you – and his medals?'

Tom Smith looked most astonished. 'You mean the man who had his medals stolen?' he asked. 'You don't mean you're trying to find the *medals*!'

'Well, that's Colin's job – but as soon as he's on to any clue we'll all help, of course,' said George.

'What an extraordinary lot you are,' said Tom Smith. 'Do you honestly think you can find those medals?'

'Well – I hope very much we can, somehow,' said George. 'For one thing, we've heard that there's a reward of five hundred pounds! The postman told us this morning, on our way here.'

'*Is* there?' said Tom, sitting up, looking very surprised. 'What will you do with that enormous sum, if you *do* find the medals?'

'Give it back to the General,' said Barbara at once. 'He's not at all well-off, you know. And he's so *terribly* upset at losing his very precious medals.'

At that very moment, a loud yell came to their ears.

'JACK! GEORGE! COOOOOO-EEEEE!'

'Gosh – that sounds like old Colin!' said George, in surprise. 'He must have seen the General, and then raced off to join us. Pity there's not much food left. Hey, COLIN! COOOOO-EEEEEE! WE'RE HERE!'

And in half a minute there was Colin, clutching his bag of food, red in the face, with a huge grin of pleasure at finding his friends. He was surprised to see a stranger with them.

'Hallo!' he said, beaming round. 'So you haven't finished your picnic. I've brought my own food, but I forgot to bring anything to drink.'

'Plenty of lemonade left,' said George, handing over a bottle. 'What a surprise, Colin! Did you do your Secret Seven job?'

'Yes,' said Colin. He glanced at Tom Smith and then at George. 'Who's your friend?' he asked.

'Tom Smith,' said George. 'He came to our rescue when some bird-nesters turned on us, and we decided to picnic together. So you saw the old General?'

Colin looked at Tom Smith again and hesitated.

'It's all right,' said George. 'We've just been telling him what the Secret Seven do – and how we hope to help the old General.'

Colin opened his plastic bag and took out a roll and tomato. He began to eat and talk at the same time.

'Yes. I saw General Branksome,' he said. 'It was pretty awful really. You see, he was so *very* upset and miserable. I hated every minute of it. And I said a silly thing – a *mad* thing – to him. I can't think why.'

'What did you say?' asked Jack, curiously.

'Well – I was so awfully sorry for him, that I found myself saying I'd find the medals and give them back to him!' said Colin. 'I mean – I actually *gave him a promise*! I can't think why!'

'Well, you *were* an idiot!' said Barbara, shocked. 'Fancy giving a promise you can't POSSIBLY keep! Anyway, I'm sure he didn't believe you.'

'Well, that's the awful part – he *did* believe me,' said Colin. 'He took my hand and shook it very hard, and said "I believe you, boy!" Oh dear – I feel so bad about it now I remember it, that I don't think I can eat anything after all.'

'Don't be an idiot,' said Jack.

'The medals were in a long case, about this size,' said Colin, measuring with his hands. 'I know because I saw the size by the empty space on the wall. Nobody has a *clue* to the thief – except that he must have very small hands, because he had to put a hand through a tiny hole in a window to get at the catch inside.'

'And that is the ONLY clue, you say?' said Tom Smith, suddenly.

'Absolutely the only clue,' said Colin, beginning to eat his roll and tomato at last. 'Gosh, I never felt so unhappy in my life as when the old General was telling me how he loved his medals. He's offered five hundred pounds reward as probably you know – but he's got hardly any money, poor old fellow.'

'I *wish* we knew where those medals were,' said Barbara, looking upset. 'Where can they be hidden? Who took them? If ONLY we knew!'

'Do you know,' said Tom Smith, suddenly, 'do you know – *I* may have a clue to their whereabouts! I'm not sure – but I *may* have!'

The four children stared at him in amazement. Then Colin reached over and pulled at his sleeve.

'Tell us, then,' he said. 'TELL US! Or tell the police. This is very, very important.'

'Well – there may be nothing in my tale,' said Tom Smith, rubbing his chin and frowning. 'Nothing at all. Still, I'll tell you, for what it's worth.'

'Go on!' said Colin, excited.

'Well, as I told your friends here, I love birds and am going to write a book about them,' said Tom Smith. 'And one of my favourite birds is the owl. Now in Bramley Woods there are many owls – they nest in the old trees here. And the other night I was here, listening to the hoots of this owl and that, lying under a tree, watching the stars shining through the branches – and suddenly . . .'

'Suddenly *what*?' asked Colin, impatiently. 'Don't keep stopping!'

'Suddenly I saw a man creep by me and go to a tree,' said Tom. 'He was carrying something. He didn't see me watching, but I could see what *he* was doing, because he had a torch.'

'And what *did* he do?' asked George, almost holding his breath.

'He lifted up a long slim box – a leather box it looked like – I saw it by the light of his torch. And he slid it into a hole in the tree-trunk – maybe a woodpecker's hole. Then he made off!'

'What did you do? Didn't you call after him? What was he like? Surely you did *some*thing?' said Colin.

'Was it – was it the box of medals?' asked Barbara.

'I don't know. It was a leather box of some sort, and about the size that holds medals for display,' said Tom.

'Did you go and look in the tree when the man had gone?' asked George. 'What did you find?'

'I went over to the tree and found the hole all right,' said Tom Smith. 'Oh yes, I did that. But my hand was far too big to put down the hole. So I don't *actually* know what the fellow slipped into that tree. Maybe it was those medals – maybe it was something else he had stolen.'

'But if it's the medals they could be taken back straight away to the General!' cried Colin. 'Show us the tree! Barbara here has small hands – she could feel down the hole and see what is there. We know the *thief* had small hands – and how clever of him to slip the stolen goods into a small hole that a large-handed person can't explore. Where *is* this tree?'

'Why should I show you?' demanded Tom Smith in a suddenly rough voice. 'What about the reward?'

'The five hundred pounds! But – surely you wouldn't take that!' said Barbara, horrified. 'You *know* the General is very poor.'

'I'll share the reward with you,' said Tom. 'Four hundred pounds to me – and a hundred pounds to you! Go on – that thief might come back at any time and get the medals he hid – he'd sell them, and they'd be melted down – and that would be the last of them.'

'You'll jolly well show us the tree and let us get the medals!' said Colin, in a fury. 'Where is it?'

'Oh, not far from here!' said Tom Smith, with a grin. 'But that's all I'll tell you! Well, what about sharing the reward?'

'Nothing doing,' said Colin, who seemed to have taken charge of the proceedings. 'Nothing doing at all! For all we know, you may be in league with some thief who hides his goods in holes in trees – some small-handed thief – but *we're* not in league with *you*. We don't intend to ask for any reward – we'll find the medals ourselves. You can't, your hands are too big – and maybe that's why the thief chooses small holes in trees to hide his goods – so that you can't rob him of the things he's stolen. What a pair you must be!'

'Now look here!' shouted Tom Smith, getting up suddenly, and looking very villainous. 'LOOK

HERE! I'll show you who's boss! I'll make you see sense!'

And he suddenly caught hold of Colin's coat-sleeve, and pulled him roughly towards him. But the boy slipped free and ran, shouting to the others.

'GET AWAY, all of you! He's dangerous. RUN!'

CHAPTER SEVEN

A VERY EXCITING PLAN

BARBARA WAS very frightened indeed, but the boys were more angry than scared. They all raced off between the trees, and didn't stop until they were out of the woods.

Then they threw themselves down on the grass that bordered the trees, and panted for breath.

'That man – won't – come after – us – will he?' panted Barbara.

'No. Too many passers-by here,' panted Jack. 'My word – who would have thought he'd turn suddenly into such a rogue!'

'Do you suppose he *really* knows where the medals are?' asked George.

'Yes. Yes, I think he does know,' said Jack. 'And I also think he *can't* get the leather case, because of the reason he gave. He really had *enormous* hands – no good for slipping into nesting-holes.'

'I'm sure that he and the thief are in league together,' said Colin. 'Tom Smith, or whoever he is, probably does the planning of robberies or burglaries, and keeps a look-out, and the other man has small hands and finds it easy to do the stealing and the hiding – and is smart enough to hide the stuff in a place that Tom Smith can't get at. Doesn't trust him!'

'What do we do now?' asked Barbara. 'I still feel scared. I want to go home.'

'Well, we simply MUST have a Secret Seven meeting at once about this,' said George. 'The others will have to know everything and we must ALL decide what to do. Let's go to Peter's. Come on.'

So away they trekked, back to the village, and went to Peter's house. They ran down the garden to the meeting-shed, and were lucky enough to find Janet there, tidying up.

'Janet! We've got news – big news!' said Colin. 'We must have a meeting as soon as possible. Where's Peter?'

'Oh dear – he won't be back till three o'clock,' said Janet. 'He's gone out with Daddy somewhere. Is it *really* important? If so, I'll tell him as soon as he gets back, and he'll telephone you.'

'No. Tell him we'll all be here at just after three, unless we hear to the contrary,' said Colin. 'That will save a lot of telephoning. Janet, we've been told where the General's medals are!'

Janet's eyes almost fell out of her head. 'Where are they?' she whispered. But just at that moment her mother appeared, and nobody said a word more about medals or thieves or anything, but just 'Well, see you about three o'clock then!'

They waved goodbye and went up the garden again to the front gate.

'I DO hope Peter will be back by three. This next meeting will be most awfully important,' said Colin.

'Well, see you all later, I hope. Gosh, I feel quite tired after all the morning's excitement!'

'I'll call in and tell Pam on my way back,' said Barbara. 'She'll be excited to know there's a most important meeting on.'

Peter did not telephone, so everyone knew that it was all right to arrive at three o'clock at the shed. Scamper was there to greet them, rushing about outside. He did so love their meetings!

'Hallo!' said Peter, welcoming the members. 'I'm longing to know the news. It must be something very important.'

'It is,' said Colin. 'More important than you can possibly imagine. Gosh – I've forgotten my badge!'

'Well – as it's such an important meeting, never mind,' said Peter, generously. Fortunately every-one had remembered the password, so there was no more trouble. Soon they were all solemnly seated on the boxes in the shed, and Peter turned to George.

'Well now – what happened to you and Barbara and Jack and Colin this morning?' he asked. 'You all look so excited. Do you REALLY know where the medals are? Janet said you did.'

'Yes. That's if a man we met in the woods this morning was telling the truth. And I rather think he was,' said George. 'He said that he knew that a man with small hands stole the medals, because he actually watched the man slipping a long, slim leather case into a bird's nesting-hole in a tree – a hole too small for this first man to get his fist into. He said it was probably a woodpecker's hole.'

'So only the small-handed man can get them,' said Peter. 'Well – this *is* news. Did he show you the tree?'

'No – he wouldn't,' said Colin. 'The only clue we got from him was that the tree wasn't very far from where we were picnicking.'

'But as there are DOZENS of trees around that isn't much help,' said Barbara. 'All we know for certain is that in one of the trees nearby, there is a hole made by a bird – or used by a bird for its nest – and into that hole the small-handed thief has slipped the case of medals. It may be half-way down the tree!'

'Looking for it would be like hunting for a needle in a haystack,' said Colin, dolefully. 'We'd NEVER find the hole.'

There was a pause. Everyone looked at everyone else.

'Well,' said Peter, at last, 'has anyone any ideas? Surely the Secret Seven can think of *some*thing between them!'

Janet spoke up, looking rather red. 'Well, *I* didn't hear what this Tom Smith said, of course, but apparently he did say that although he knew the tree, he couldn't get out the medals hidden there because his hands were too big to go into the hole. Well then – what is he going to do? I bet he's going to hide and wait till the other man comes to get them – and then he's going to go for him and snatch the medals! Well – why shouldn't one of *us* go and hide too, and wait to see which tree it is? Scamper could go as well, and . . .'

'And might scare them off, so that we could get at the tree!' cried Peter, in delight. 'Janet, you're too clever for words!'

'Well – I was going to suggest that we should ask the *police* to go and watch as well,' said Janet.

'Oh – I see. No – I think they'd say the reward would have to be paid out,' said Peter. 'And it might go to a police charity or something. Not that I'm against that – but we know the old General is poor, and can't afford to pay out five hundred pounds. If *we* find the medals ourselves, and actually take them out of the tree, the reward is safe. We can say "No thank you, we don't want any reward" – and that's that.'

'Anyway, the police are so BIG,' said Barbara. 'They'd be sure to be seen. We're small. We could shin up a tree and hide in the leaves like birds!'

'And we'd be *quite* safe with Scamper,' said Pam. 'Wouldn't we, Scamper?'

'WUFF,' said Scamper at once, very loudly. He wagged his tail and looked very proud. So *he* was to be in this adventure too! Ha – what a tale to tell the dog next door!

Everyone suddenly became very excited. '*I* shall go,' said Colin. 'After all, *I* was given the job of solving the medals robbery.'

'And I shall go because I thought of the idea,' said Janet.

'And *I* shall go because I'm head of the Secret Seven,' said Peter.

'Look – don't be silly – we can't *all* go!' said George. 'The thief would spot us – or hear us – as soon as he came near us.'

'How do we know he'd come near us?' asked Janet. 'The tree might be quite far away from anyone.'

'We *know* it's not far from where we picnicked,' said Colin. 'Look – don't let's be silly. We shall mess things up if we *all* go. And I'm not *really* sure about

Scamper – he might bark too soon and scare off the thief before he came to the right tree.'

'There's something in that, Colin,' said Peter. 'I think if we take Scamper, he should be some way away, held on the lead by one of us – and not until somebody blew a whistle – me, for instance – would Scamper be allowed to race up and join the fun!'

So they talked – and talked – and planned – and grew more and more excited. At last everything was arranged and settled. Peter repeated their plans for the last time.

'We tell no one at all about this. We meet here when it's dark. Bring warm scarves in case it's cold – and torches – and PLEASE check to see that your battery is good. You don't want to be left suddenly in the dark.'

'It will be moonlight, don't forget,' said Pam.

'I know,' said Peter. 'But clouds may darken the moon – and in any case it will be dark in the wood. Now – when we get to the woods, we keep absolute silence, unless we are able to whisper right into some-body's ear. Understood?'

'Yes,' whispered everyone, imagining themselves to be already in the woods.

'Each of us hides – either up a tree – or in a bush – and keeps watch on all the trees around,' went on Peter. 'Colin will point out where the picnic was held, and then we shall each spread around, and hide in different places, so that if anyone comes that way, one or other of us will see him. There will be no giggling, no noise of any sort that you can help. Understood?'

'Yes,' said everyone again, and the girls felt a little shiver going down their backs. This really was too exciting for words!

'We watch to see what tree the thief goes to, to get the medals from,' went on Peter. 'Then I'll let loose old Scamper, who will go for him and scare him away – and we will examine the tree and remove the medals ourselves!'

'I really do think this is about the most exciting adventure we've ever had,' said Barbara, with a catch in her voice. 'It's quite *dangerous*!'

'Not if you do as you're told,' said Peter. 'And mind – if any one of you begins to feel scared, *keep still in your hiding-place* – don't come out, for goodness' sake – you might spoil everything! Well – that's all. We'll now close this meeting. Remember to be here punctually as soon as it's dark enough. We shan't wait for anyone who is late.'

Everyone at once determined to be on the early side. It would be dreadful to be left out of this most exciting and thrilling adventure!

'If *only* we can find those medals!' said Colin to himself, as he went home. 'And I can take them back to the old General and see his face. I honestly think I want that more than anything in this world!'

Well, keep your fingers crossed, Colin. This isn't an easy adventure – anything may happen, so keep on your guard – and good luck to all the Secret Seven!

CHAPTER EIGHT

HOLD YOUR BREATH, SECRET SEVEN

SUSIE, JACK's irritating sister, was very curious that night, when she saw Jack fitting a new battery into his torch.

'Are you going out tonight?' she demanded. 'Where are you going?'

'Where I go is nothing to do with *you*,' said Jack crossly. 'Always poking your nose in where you're not wanted.'

'You're going somewhere with the Secret Seven, I know you are,' said Susie. 'Tell me. Go on – you *might* tell me!'

'Certainly NOT!' said Jack, exasperated.

'Oh – then you *are* going somewhere,' said Susie.

'I just *wish* you were a boy,' said Jack. 'I'd give you such a punch. Stop questioning me.'

'Well – I shall follow you,' said the annoying Susie. 'And I shall get Binkie to come with me.'

'You'll do nothing of the sort!' said Jack, horrified. 'This is a matter for the Secret Seven and no one else. Keep out of it!'

'Well, tell me what it is, then,' said Susie.

Jack stamped away and shut himself into his room. Bother Susie! She had a real nose for anything in the way of a Secret Seven adventure. *Would* she follow him – with that wretched, twitchy-nosed Binkie friend of hers? Well – he'd start pretty early, then he would have time to shake them off.

All the Secret Seven were busy examining their torches that afternoon and going over Peter's instructions in their minds. Scamper couldn't imagine why Peter and Janet were so restless. The time went so slowly for them – it seemed as if the evening would never come!

'Now Scamper, you'll have to be careful to do EXACTLY what you're told,' said Peter to the eager spaniel. 'You'll probably have to leap at a man and hold him – but don't bite, you understand. And please do be careful not to make *any* noise until I give the word. Understood?'

'Wuff,' said Scamper, happily. Of course he understood!

It seemed a long time to all the Seven before the evening came. Darkness seemed to be later than ever! But then great clouds blew up and the dark night descended quite suddenly. Peter and Janet fidgeted over their supper, and their mother wondered what was the matter.

'Do you feel quite well?' she asked.

'Goodness, yes!' said Peter in alarm. 'Er – the Secret Seven are having a late-ish meeting tonight, Mother, so, as you're going out with Daddy, we'd better say good night to you now. See you in the morning.'

'Well, dear, don't let the meeting go on *too* late,' said his mother. 'Daddy and I will be in just before midnight, I hope – you'll be *fast* asleep hours before that.'

Peter was most relieved to think that his parents were going out. He and Janet were all ready – torches in order, sweets to suck while they were waiting in their hiding-places and warm scarves in case the night proved cold.

The Seven all came together quietly as soon as it was dark. Torches shone out in the garden as the members went down to the shed.

'All here?' asked Peter. 'Yes. Good. All torches alight? Good. Warm scarves? Good!'

They set off together, Scamper at Peter's heels. The moon came out as soon as it grew darker, but they lost its friendly light when they came to the woods, and it seemed very shadowy among the trees.

'Is that footsteps I hear somewhere behind us?' said Peter, suddenly stopping. 'I thought I heard a crack as if someone some way behind had stepped on a twig.'

Jack frowned. Gosh – surely it wasn't Susie and Binkie. No – he really didn't think Susie had seen him slip out of the house. As Peter heard no more suspicious sounds they all went on again, very quietly indeed.

Barbara took Pam's arm. She wasn't scared, but she just thought she'd like to feel someone really close to her. Pam was pleased too! This really was a proper adventure!

Scamper sniffed here and there as he went along. He was delighted to go out for a walk with all the Seven in the dark of night! They came to Bramley Woods, and were soon at the place where they had picnicked.

'Now – we know that the tree where the medals are hidden is somewhere not far off,' whispered Peter. 'We'd all better get into our hiding-places. Anywhere you like, so long as you're hidden. Spread out a bit, so that our eyes can cover a good many trees around here.'

Gradually the Seven disappeared, Scamper too. Peter climbed a tree, and so did Jack. Janet found a fairly comfortable bush, through whose leaves she could easily peep. Pam lay down in some high ferns, hoping nobody would walk over her. Barbara squeezed into the very middle of a bush, where she was so well hidden that not one single S.S. member knew where she was.

I could almost go to sleep here, she thought. But, of course, she was much too excited even to shut her eyes!

Colin and George climbed on to a great branch of an old oak-tree, and lay along it, whispering to one another. Scamper lay in some ferns at the foot of Peter's tree, his ears pricked for the slightest whisper from his master on the branch above.

Nobody could see anybody else. That was good, thought Peter. Very good. It meant that no intruder would see them either.

An owl suddenly hooted from a tree nearby and all the Secret Seven jumped violently. Scamper growled at once, and Peter hissed at him. Scamper stopped growling and lay down again, his ears pricked. What did that bird mean by hooting at him like that?

A rabbit came from a hole and lolloped lazily across the grass. Everyone watched it in delight. Then it was joined by another, and the two danced around, running here and there, jumping and playing. The moon shone down on them, and Scamper shut his eyes in despair. Rabbits so close – and he dared not run at them! It was too much!

Then a squirrel came bounding along the branch where Colin and George lay, and stopped in alarm to see the boys there. Neither of them moved, and in the end the squirrel decided they were part of the tree, and ran lightly over them, sniffing at their faces inquisitively.

'Oooh – don't tickle!' whispered Colin, and the squirrel leapt away in surprise.

Poor Jack suddenly felt a sneeze coming. His nose tickled and he swallowed violently to keep the sneeze back. It swelled and swelled – and at last exploded into a great big WHOOSHOO!, sending the rabbits down their holes in fright, and making the other Secret Seven members jump almost out of their skins. Peter, not far from Jack, almost fell out of his tree!

'Idiot!' he said, in a loud whisper. 'Don't do that again for goodness' sake. I nearly fell to the ground.'

'I couldn't help it,' whispered back Jack, in an aggrieved voice. 'I nearly fell down myself. I say – isn't the moon bright!'

'SHHH!' said Peter, fiercely, afraid that everyone would soon join in the conversation.

There was dead silence once more. Then the wind began to blow a little, and small sh-sh-sh noises were everywhere. The owl descended near Pam's ferns and hooted suddenly again. Pam leapt up with a shriek, making everyone jump in alarm.

'Pam! You'd better go home!' said Peter, in a fierce whisper. 'Go on. Go home!'

Pam subsided into her ferns again, almost in tears. She was NOT going home. Bother that owl! Why did it have to hoot almost in her ear?

Peace descended once again. The owl had gone. The rabbits had shot back into their holes, frightened by the hoot. Nobody sneezed. Nobody coughed. But somebody gave a little yawn!

'SHHH!' hissed Peter. 'I think there's somebody coming.'

That made everyone lie as still as could be. Hearts began to beat fast, and Pam couldn't help hoping that hers wasn't really as loud as it sounded. Bump-bump-bump, it went against her chest.

Yes. Somebody *was* coming! All the Seven – and Scamper too – could hear the sound of soft footsteps padding through the wood. Little twigs cracked now and again, and the newcomer cleared his throat once or twice. Who was it? The thief who had hidden the medals? Tom Smith? Or just a night-walker?

It was *Tom Smith*! There he was, walking in the moonlight, his arms, with their big hands, swinging by his side. Had he come to hunt for the hidden medals – but no, his hands were too big to seek for them in a tree-hole. He would have to wait till the other fellow came, the small-handed man who stole the medals, and hid them in a hole in some tree.

Tom Smith whistled softly as he walked between the trees, passing so near Pam in the ferns that she was half afraid he would tread on her. Then he stopped and looked around carefully. He was not looking for the Secret Seven, of course, though each of them felt that he was, and cowered more closely in their hiding-places.

He's come to wait for the thief, thought Peter, peering down from his tree. My guess is that he'll hide somewhere, and watch to see if the man goes to a certain tree. My goodness – this is exciting!

Yes – it was! Hold your breath a little longer, Seven. Lie quiet, Scamper. Tom Smith is in hiding now – waiting, waiting – waiting – for somebody else to come.

CHAPTER NINE

THE SEVEN ARE IN TROUBLE

TOM SMITH went to a broad-trunked oak-tree, and hid himself behind it. He did not know that Colin and George were up in the same tree, just above his head. The boys hardly dared to breathe. Scamper lay still not far off, crouched on the ground, as flat as he could make himself. Everyone was very still – yet inwardly tingling with excitement – waiting to see what was going to happen next.

There came a sudden bark – but not from Scamper! All the Seven pricked up their ears at once. Another dog was coming – maybe the small-handed thief was bringing him – for protection! Perhaps he feared that Tom Smith might be lying in wait for him – as indeed he was.

There came a low, soft whistling, and someone walked into the moonlit patch of grass not far from Pam. Behind him was a large dog.

Phew – an Alsatian! thought Peter. Let's hope he doesn't sniff out Scamper – he'd eat him up in no time. Gosh – I don't much like this!

The Alsatian suddenly growled. Had he smelt Scamper – or some of the Seven?

'Shut up, Nabber,' ordered the man with him. 'There's no one about. You can hear rabbits, that's all.'

The man went across the moonlit patch towards a group of big trees, Nabber close behind him, still growling deep down in his throat. Then the watching children saw Tom Smith creep out from his hiding-place. The Alsatian stopped, turned his head, and growled ferociously.

Tom Smith shouted to the other man. 'I'm here, Wily! You get those medals and we'll talk. There's a fine reward out for them now – we'll share!'

'No, we won't,' said Wily, and laughed. 'Ha – I might have thought you'd be on the watch for me. You clear off, else I'll set Nabber on you.'

'Nabber won't touch me,' shouted Tom. 'He knows me. You get those things – go on, now.'

'Come and get them yourself!' shouted back Wily. 'Here they are, see – down in this tree-hole. Come and stick your big fist in and take them if you want them!'

'You know I can't get my great hand in there,' said Tom, fiercely. 'You were going to double-cross me, weren't you – come here in the dark and take the things out of their hiding-place without me knowing. Oh no, Wily – you just take them out here and now, and hand them over to me. Go on! You don't want to fight a big fellow like me, do you? My fists would make twelve of your dainty little hands.'

Wily began to walk away from the tree he was near. He laughed, and it was such a mocking sound that Tom Smith lost his temper. There came the sound of a loud smack, and lo and behold, little Wily was on the ground! The Alsatian at once flew at Tom Smith, and down *he* went on the ground!

The children watched everything in fear and astonishment. The only one among them who was enjoying this battle was Scamper. How he longed to rush in and help that big Alsatian.

He couldn't stop himself from barking joyfully. WUFF-WUFF-WUFF!

At once the Alsatian lifted his head and glanced round, amazed. Tom Smith leapt up, and the other man called to Nabber. 'Get that dog!'

Nabber rushed at Scamper and bowled him completely over. But Scamper thought it was a game, leapt up, and danced round the big Alsatian, giving happy little whines. He didn't often have the chance of a game with such a big dog!

Peter dropped down from his tree, and so did Jack, both afraid that Scamper might get bitten. 'Scamper! Heel! Come to heel!' ordered Peter. 'SCAMPERRRRRR!'

Nabber the Alsatian was amazed to see two boys suddenly dropping from a tree – and as for Tom Smith and Wily, they stared as if they couldn't believe their eyes. First a spaniel – and now two boys! What on earth was happening in the woods tonight!

Scamper was still darting happily round the surprised Alsatian, who was young enough to enjoy a silly game himself. The two men came over to Peter and Jack, and Tom shook Peter roughly.

'What are you doing here? Snooping? That dog might have bitten you badly – and serve you jolly well right!'

'Take your hand off me!' said Peter, fiercely. 'Yes, we're snooping! *You* told my friends this morning about the medals and how your small-handed friend had hidden them in a hole in a tree somewhere about here. So we came to have a look round, thinking it would be a good thing if *we* got them. They would be handed over to their rightful owner then!'

'And what's more we're going straight back to the police station,' said Jack. 'I've no doubt that the police will soon catch you both.'

Tom Smith suddenly snatched at Peter's arm, pulled the boy towards him, and looked at his right hand. 'Come on!' he said. '*You're* going to get that case of medals out of the tree for me! Your hand's quite small enough to get right down into that hole. Come on!'

He dragged Peter towards the trees where he and Wily had stood arguing. Scamper flew at him and tried to bite him through his thick trousers. He kicked out and Scamper yelped.

'Don't you dare to kick my dog!' said Peter, furiously. Tom kicked out again, and once more Scamper yelped. That was too much for Janet to bear, and she suddenly leapt out of the nearby bush in which she was hiding, and raced over to the whining spaniel.

'Scamper! DEAR Scamper! Are you hurt?'

Tom Smith and Wily were amazed to see a girl rushing up. 'Look here – how many more are there of you?' said Tom, looking round. 'What *are* you kids doing here so late at night?'

The rest of the Seven couldn't bear to be in hiding any longer, and to the utter astonishment of the two men, Pam jumped up from the ferns she lay in, Barbara pressed out of her bush, and Colin and George dropped down from their oak-tree.

'What *is* all this?' said Wily, taken aback by the sudden appearance of so many children.

'It's the kids belonging to that silly club they told me about this morning,' groaned Tom Smith. 'Look – be sensible, Wily – get that case out of the tree, and we'll both be off.'

'No. I don't trust you,' said Wily, sulkily.

'Right. I'll make this boy get it for me then,' said Tom Smith, angrily, and pulled Peter to a big, very old tree. There was a hole a good way up the trunk, and he tried to thrust Peter's hand into it, shining a torch so that the boy could see what he was doing.

'Don't!' said Peter, fiercely. 'My hand's too big. Stop it! You're grazing all the skin off. I tell you, it WON'T GO IN!'

'All right!' said Tom, and he grabbed Pam, who was watching in horror. 'Ha – here's a nice small hand. Go on, now – take out the case, girl. Do as you're told.'

'Stand away. You're scaring her,' said Peter, angrily. 'Look, she's trembling. She'll find it much easier if you stand right away. Won't you, Pam?'

He gave Pam a nudge. She pretended to cry, and said, in a shaky voice: 'Stand behind me, Peter. I'm frightened. Keep those men right away. My hand is shaking so much I can't even put it into the hole while they're near me.'

'All right, all right, we'll stand away,' said Tom. 'Now go on – stick in your hand, feel about for the case, and pull it out very gently.'

Peter whispered in Pam's ear. 'Get the case out quickly, and give it to me, but *pretend you're still feeling for it.*'

Pam put her hand into the hole, felt the case at once and slid it out easily. Peter took it quietly and opened it. He slid the medals into his pocket, talking loudly to Pam all the time, hoping that the men's attention was elsewhere.

'That's right. Easy now. Got it, Pam? Slide it out carefully, carefully! Those men aren't near you. Don't be afraid! Good girl – here comes the case!'

At these words the men were immediately beside Peter, who handed Tom the empty case, praying that they wouldn't open it. Tom, afraid that Wily would try to snatch it, popped it promptly into his pocket. He turned to go, but Wily caught his arm.

'Wait! What about these kids? They'll race home and tell the police. We need a good start, Tom. And let me tell you this – I'm going to keep you by my side until you hand me half those medals.'

'Oh come now – we can't tie the kids up, Wily,' said Tom. 'No rope, for one thing.'

'Well – we'll leave Nabber on guard,' said Wily. 'He'll nip any child who tries to run. He'll stay here till morning, if I tell him to.'

'Fine, fine,' said Tom, pleased. 'Tell him, then.'

'Stay, Nabber, stay. All night see, all night. Stay, Nabber!' ordered Wily. 'Round up the kids for me. And STAY!'

'You can't do a thing like that!' cried Peter. But that was exactly what Wily did do! He and Tom Smith set off at a smart walk, and left Nabber behind with the Seven. Nabber whined – but he was absolutely obedient.

He rounded up the seven children, *and* Scamper, and lay down near them, watching warily for any movement.

'This is absolutely the limit!' said Colin, angrily. 'What on earth will all our parents think when they find we're not home? They'll be worried stiff. I'M not going to stay here all night long, anyway.'

And up he jumped and began to walk away down the path. But Nabber was after him in a jiffy. He caught the boy by his coat-sleeve and held on, pulling him backwards to the others.

'It's no good, Colin,' called Peter. 'He's trained to do this sort of thing. We'll only be dragged back, and maybe nipped if we try to get away.'

'Well, anyway *Peter*'s got the gold medals,' suddenly said Pam, and laughed. 'The men have only got the empty box! Wasn't it clever of Peter to make out I was so frightened, and how lucky they didn't watch what we were doing?'

'Whatever *do* you mean?' said Janet, in wonder.

Peter took out one of the big medals from his pocket and held it up in the moonlight, laughing. 'Good old Pam! She acted up like anything. She was so quick that I was able to open the box and remove the medals – then shut it, and give it to the men quite empty.'

And then the Seven began to laugh. How they laughed! They had outwitted two thieves and a big Alsatian, and had sent away the men with an empty box – and there was Peter with all the medals safely in his pocket! Well done indeed, Secret Seven! But oh dear, it's NOT very funny to spend a night in the dark woods, with a nasty cold little wind roaming round. And Nabber is *sure* to have you, if you try to escape!

CHAPTER TEN

A LONG, COLD WAIT

THE SEVEN made themselves as comfortable as they could in the ferns. Scamper lay down beside Peter and Janet, and soon they were quite glad of the warmth of his body, for the night-wind came creeping round, cold and draughty.

'I'm AWFULLY cold!' complained Pam, after a while. 'I really am. Oooh – how I'd love a hot-water bottle.'

'We'd better all get close together,' said Colin. 'Look – you girls get in the middle and we boys will sit round you. That will keep off the wind a little.'

'Thanks, Colin,' said the girls, and were soon squashed closely together, with the boys sitting round them. Peter held Scamper on his lap then, and he really did feel as warm as a hot-water bottle.

'I'll have to lend you round, Scamper,' said Peter. 'You're so nice and warm. You must go and warm up everyone in turn.'

Nabber the Alsatian took very little notice of them. He sat nearby with his back to them, as if watching for Wily his master to return. But at the least sound or movement from the Seven, his ears shot back, and he listened for any sign of escape. Once, when Peter got up to shift his position a little, and make himself more comfortable, the big dog ran to the group of children, growling and showing his white teeth. It would certainly be no use to try and escape. Nobody would get far with Nabber after him.

'All right, Nabber. We aren't idiotic enough to try and fool you,' said Colin. 'You can go to sleep if you want to!'

But Nabber didn't go to sleep. No – if he had to lie there all night long, he wouldn't close his eyes for a single minute. Scamper closed his, though. He was tired and anxious – something was wrong, and he couldn't do anything about it. He found his eyes closing, gave a little sigh, and went to sleep – but he opened his eyes soon enough when a daring rabbit hopped out of its hole and sniffed at the silent little company.

'Those men will have *plenty* of time to get away,' groaned Peter. 'By the time morning comes, and this Alsatian leaves us, the two men will be miles away.'

'I wonder when they'll discover that the medal case is empty,' said Pam. 'I'd like to be there then. It would be funny to see their faces.'

'I only hope they don't discover too soon that the case is empty, and come racing back to find what we've done with the medals,' said Janet.

'That's not at all a pleasant thought,' said Peter, sitting up straight. 'I hadn't realised they might come back. Gosh – we'll have to look out. Scamper, keep your ears pricked and growl if you hear those fellows returning.'

'Wuff!' said Scamper, at once, and sat up very straight. No more sleep for him!

Half an hour went by, seeming like two hours. The Seven were colder still and Pam shivered so much that the others complained that she made them shiver too.

'Good thing Peter told us to bring warm scarves,' said Barbara. 'At least our necks are warm.'

'I've wrapped *my* scarf round my feet,' said Janet. 'They felt like ice.'

Nabber the Alsatian suddenly rose to his feet, his sharp ears pricked to the utmost. He had been lying some way from the children, nose on paws, eyeing them all in case anyone made a sudden move to escape. Scamper suddenly sat up too.

'Hallo – the dogs have heard something,' said Colin. 'See their ears? Mine feel as if they're pricking up too, but I can't hear anything yet.'

Nabber gave a low growl, but Scamper kept quiet. A sound came in the distance, and Nabber growled again.

'Sounded like a bicycle bell!' said Colin. 'Funny. Who would be cycling to Bramley Woods as late as this?'

Nabber growled again, and looked back at the Seven as if to say 'Now then – not a sound or a movement, see!' Scamper whined loudly, which astonished the Seven. Why whine instead of growling?

The bell sound came again – yes – it *was* a bicycle bell! The Seven cheered up at once!

'Look – if it's a late-night cyclist, coming this way, we'll all yell our heads off,' said Peter. 'Then maybe he'll stop and we can tell him what's happened.'

'But how can he stop Nabber guarding us?' asked Pam. 'We'll have to warn him about the Alsatian. It would be awful if Nabber went for him.'

'Gosh, yes. I didn't think of that,' said Peter. 'Bother! We can't risk his being bitten.'

Everyone's heart sank. They all listened intently for sounds to come nearer. Ah – there was the ringing of the bell again – *two* bells, surely? So *more* than one person was coming? Perhaps Peter could yell to stop them coming too near – and shout to them to get help of some sort, and explain about the Alsatian. Oh dear – it was all very difficult.

Now *voices* could be heard – children's voices, not grown-ups'! How odd! What children would be cycling at this time of night in lonely roads through the woods?

Jack suddenly gave a shout and leapt to his feet. 'I can hear SUSIE's voice!' he yelled. 'And Binkie's with her! I'm sure it's them!'

'What in the world are they doing cycling here at this time of night?' said Peter, astounded.

'Susie *knew* we had something exciting on tonight,' said Jack. 'You know how snoopy she is. All right, all right, Nabber, I'm not going to run away, I'm only standing up. Go and lie down, there's a good dog. Oh Peter, I bet Susie went and looked at my notebook and saw my note there, about meeting in the woods this evening. She threatened to follow me!'

'Well – for *once* in a way I shall be very glad to see that sister of yours, *and* her silly friend, Binkie,' said Peter. 'It DOES sound like their voices. Let's all yell Susie's name.'

And so, echoing through the tall trees overhead and down all the little paths Susie's name went on, on and on in the night. 'Soo-sy, Soooooo-sy, Soo-soo-soo-sy!'

Nabber was amazed at all the sudden shouting. He sat and stared at the yelling children, wondering what to do. Well – they weren't running away – they were only shouting. Nabber lay down again and put his head on his paws. But Scamper went wild with excitement!

He had heard the girls' voices too, and recognised them at once. He raced away from the Seven, down the path, in the direction of the voices. Nabber looked after him, but didn't stop him. Scamper wasn't one of the children. He didn't have to guard *him*!

The voices *were* Susie's and Binkie's! How surprising – and how wonderful! Peter sat and listened to the sound of the voices coming nearer. Never, never had he ever guessed that he would be glad to hear that exasperating Susie's voice!

The two girls had heard Susie's name being called and were now shouting back. 'We're coming! Where are you? Is anything wrong with you? Why are you here so late?'

'We're HERE! HERE!' yelled back the others.

'Come and meet us!' shouted Susie. 'Or flash your torches. It's so dark.'

'Susie, there's an Alsatian dog guarding us. Be careful!' shouted Jack. 'Don't come too near.'

The lights of the two bicycles were now like eyes, coming nearer and nearer. Nabber stood up and began to growl, all his hackles rising on his neck. Jack was afraid for the two girls.

'Don't come any nearer!' he yelled. 'Susie, do you hear me! Get off your bikes and stop. The dog will go for you, if you don't.'

'WHAT DOG?' yelled Susie. But she did as she was told, stopped, jumped off her bicycle, and flashed a torch over towards the Seven. 'Gosh – here you all are, bunched together – you must be frozen!'

Binkie jumped off her bicycle too, and wheeled it towards the Seven. At once Nabber growled and ran out towards her, showing a set of dazzling white teeth. Binkie was terrified.

'STAND STILL!' shouted Peter, and Binkie stood as if she was turned into stone.

'What's up?' called Susie. 'Why is that great dog guarding you? What's happened?'

'Can't tell you now!' yelled back Jack. 'But you can help us a lot. Go and tell the police we're here and can't get away because of this Alsatian. They may know of a dog-handler who can come along and deal with him. Thank goodness you came after us – first time I've ever been glad you're such nuisances!'

'Now don't you talk like that to *us*!' began Binkie, wheeling her bicycle a little closer. Nabber gave such a horrible growl that she shrieked in fright and went backwards very quickly indeed. Scamper gave a small piteous whine. He was very, very unhappy to think that he wasn't big enough to fight this determined Alsatian, and send him running.

'Jack!' called Susie. 'We'll do as you say – and we'll be as quick as we can. Goodbye for now!'

'Well – Susie *can* be sensible after all,' said Colin, surprised. 'I always thought she was the world's prize idiot.'

'She's all right really,' said Jack. 'She'll go straight to the police and they'll be here in a jiffy. Susie *can* be really sensible when she wants to.'

The Seven listened to the sound of the girls' shrill voices getting farther and farther away. The bicycle bells rang once or twice, and then no more could be heard. Scamper gave a small whine, and then flopped down on the ground again.

'Cheer up, Scamper. We shan't have to be here all night, after all,' said Peter, stroking the soft silky head. 'I just hope that Nabber has the sense not to fly at a policeman. He's the sort of dog I'd much rather have as a friend than as an enemy.'

Nabber lay down when the two girls had gone and gave a sigh, as if to say 'What a nuisance these children are! Fancy having to guard them for hours!'

'Cheer up, Nabber!' said Colin. 'All nights have to come to an end. This one may end sooner than you think.'

Nabber lay full length and stared at Colin, listening. Then he gave a most enormous yawn, turned round, and sat with his back to them all.

'Doesn't think much of us, that's plain,' said Janet. 'But I like him. Let's sing, to cheer ourselves up.'

So they all sang at the tops of their voices, much to Nabber's amazement. He lifted his head and joined in with the most enormous howls, which made everyone laugh so much that the singing came to an end.

'We'd better listen for the police now,' said Peter. 'They should be here at any moment. Listen – what's that? It's the sound of a car – HURRAY!'

CHAPTER ELEVEN

NABBER MEETS HIS MATCH

YES – it was certainly a car, and it sounded a powerful one. It had extremely good headlights too, which lighted up the woods in rather a weird manner.

It came to a stop just about where the two girls had stood with their bicycles. Then a stentorian voice shouted, 'Are you children there?'

'YES!' yelled back Peter. 'But we daren't move because of the Alsatian dog. He's guarding us. Can't you hear him barking?'

As soon as the police car had switched off its engine, the police heard Nabber barking. What a bark! It echoed all through the wood!

Then suddenly a dark van came up the woodland road, and drew to a halt just behind the police car.

'That's a *police* van!' said Jack, excited. 'Hey, what a thing to happen to the Secret Seven! Police to the rescue. Gosh – what's that?'

A great clamour had broken out from the van behind the car, and immediately Nabber went quite mad. He galloped round and round the bunch of children, barking and growling in a most unpleasant way. For some reason Scamper joined him, adding his wuffs to the noise.

'This must be a *dream*, I think,' said Barbara, rubbing her eyes. 'It can't be *really* happening!'

But it *was* all real – and so were the policemen that jumped from the first car, and made their way towards the Seven. At once Nabber growled ferociously, and bared his teeth.

'Look out, for goodness' sake – he'll come for you if you walk any nearer!' yelled Colin. 'He's supposed to be guarding us till daylight.'

The two policemen stopped at once, and one called back to the van. 'Big Alsatian loose here, Harris.

He'll have to be rounded up before we do anything more. Get your two out.'

'*Two!* Have they brought *two* Alsatians?' said George, in delight. 'Gosh – we're going to see some fun!'

A man stepped from the dark van, holding two enormous, excited, panting Alsatians on a strong lead. They strained at the great leather strap, barking. Then one smelt the scent of the Alsatian near the children, and gave such a blood-curdling growl that everyone's heart began to beat very fast indeed.

'Oh please – they won't *fight* Nabber, will they?' shouted Janet. 'He's not a bad dog, really he isn't. Don't let him get hurt, will you?'

'He won't get hurt, missie, if he behaves sensibly,' called the man holding back the two dogs. 'And keep that spaniel close to you, will you? Don't let him move if you can help it. And all of you keep absolutely silent, and absolutely still while my dogs get to work.'

Janet promptly took Scamper, who was quivering with excitement, on to her knee and held him as tightly as she could. She needn't have worried – Scamper had no intention of getting mixed up with dogs so much bigger than he was!

The seven children never forgot what happened in the next few minutes. Not one of them had seen a trained dog-handler at work – dogs and man understood one another so well that it seemed as if the two police dogs knew what was in their master's mind almost before he had given a command.

'I'm going to let my dogs go now,' shouted the dog-handler. 'Don't scream or shout, you children. They won't harm you at all – they won't even notice you. They'll just round up that other dog, and bring him to me.'

In dead silence, the children watched everything in the light given by the car-lamps. Janet held Scamper so tightly that he whined. The two police dogs pattered slowly up to where they were all sitting, and fixed their eyes on Nabber, who now crouched behind a big tree, his tongue hanging out, his eyes gleaming in the car-lights. As he watched the two dogs, he began to growl.

'Round him up!' shouted the dog-handler. 'Get to work, Sasha! Now!'

And at the word 'NOW!' Sasha gave a great leap forward, then sideways, and was suddenly right behind the surprised Nabber.

'Now you, Vanya!' yelled the man. And there was the second dog, facing Nabber, ready to fly at him, whichever way he turned. Nabber tried to dodge this way and that, showing his teeth all the time – and then suddenly he leapt right over the dog facing him, and disappeared into the woods.

'FETCH HIM!' yelled the handler. There was the noise of a scrimmage in the ferns some way away, and then Nabber came flying back to the children. He leapt right over the whole bunch of them as they sat there, alarmed – and then up raced Sasha and Vanya, leaping over them too.

'Quite a circus!' whispered Peter to Jack, as they watched the three dogs tearing round, leaping, dodging, Sasha and Vanya snapping at Nabber, sometimes disappearing through the trees for a few seconds, but always coming back to the handler, who still shouted instructions to them from time to time.

Quite suddenly Sasha leapt on Nabber from behind, and got him by the scruff of his neck. Nabber howled and tried to get free. Then he began to whine piteously.

'Right. Drop him, Sasha!' said the handler. 'Bring him to me. DROP HIM! He won't run away any more. Nabber – that's your name, isn't it? Come here, then. Good dog, then, come here.'

And to the children's intense surprise, the fierce Nabber, head hanging down, limping a little on one leg, went obediently to the dog-handler. On each side of him, came Sasha and Vanya, their tails wagging victoriously. The man patted Nabber on the head, fondled his ears, and then, as Nabber rolled over in delight, tickled his tummy. Sasha and Vanya watched solemnly, and waited for their own reward of pats and praise.

'WELL!' said George, watching in amazement. 'Wouldn't I love to be able to handle dogs like that? I'll jolly well train to be a dog-handler as soon as I'm old enough.'

A police officer came up to the children. 'Well, now the fun's over, you'd better see if you can all squash into our car and we'll run you home,' he said. 'Those two girls who came to tell us about the trouble you were in, will be glad to know you're safe – and so will your parents, I should think. But now – how was it you were here at night, with that dog on guard so that you were his prisoners? And whose dog is he?'

And then, in the car, the whole tale came out, of course – about the stolen medals – the man called

Tom Smith who had told them they were hidden in a tree-hole too small for his big hand to slip into – and how they, the Seven, had had the idea of coming to find the medals themselves – and had run into trouble.

By this time they were almost out of the woods, and in the lane that led to the main road. The police officer had listened carefully to the story, without interrupting. 'Do you know the names of these men – and can you give us a description?' he asked. 'I think they're the two that we are after for a series of burglaries – and other things!'

'Well – one said his name was Tom Smith – and he called the other man Wily,' began Peter – and then stopped suddenly as they passed by a little inn called the Hare and Hounds. He caught at the policeman's arm.

'Could you stop the car? I rather think that was Tom Smith rushing out of the front door of that inn, with Wily after him. I'm pretty sure Wily was shouting, too. I expect they've quarrelled – about the medals!'

And then, to the policeman's surprise, Peter began to laugh and laugh. No wonder – for he had the medals *safely in his own pocket*! But the police didn't know that – yet! Peter was determined that the old General should have the medals delivered to him personally by *Colin* – for that was what Colin had promised the old man.

The car slowed and stopped just by the two men. Tom was fending off Wily, and both men were shouting angrily.

The police van in front noticed that the second car had stopped, and it stopped too, and reversed. The police officer in the second vehicle jumped out and ran to the driver of the first one.

'We'll pick up these two fellows for questioning,' he said. 'Hurry up. I rather think we've got the men we've been looking for. That Alsatian in your van – Nabber – belongs to one of them.'

And then, to Tom Smith's surprise, and to Wily's horror, the two policemen bore down on them and took them firmly to the van, where they were put in with the three Alsatians. Nabber was too thrilled for words to see his master, and covered him with licks. Wily was amazed to see his dog. 'I'm dreaming!' he said, stroking Nabber. 'Yes, I'm dreaming! Nabber, I left you with those kids – and here you are with the police. Yes, I'm dreaming. Good thing you're in my dream, too, Nabber – you'll look after me, won't you?'

'I'm beginning to feel *I'm* dreaming too,' said Janet, as the two cars went on their way again, with seven children, four dogs, two policemen, a dog-handler and two prisoners. 'Let's hope we don't have to pick up anyone or anything else!'

The two cars swept into the village and stopped at a corner. 'Now you kids tumble out,' said the police officer. 'Time you were all in bed! We'll be round tomorrow to see you. Tell your parents there's nothing to worry about – we're very pleased with our night's work. I only hope we'll find the old General's medals in Tom Smith's pocket.'

You won't! They're still in *Peter*'s pocket! Only ONE person is going to give back the medals to General Branksome – and that's Colin, of course!

CHAPTER TWELVE

WELL DONE, SECRET SEVEN

ALL THE children's parents were extremely relieved to see them safely home. They each said the same thing.

'WHERE have you been at this time of night? And WHAT have you been doing? You are NOT to do this kind of thing – we were TERRIBLY worried!'

Susie had also been very worried. She was very glad indeed to see her brother Jack coming in at the front gate. She had been watching anxiously for him. Binkie was with her, also watching.

'There he is!' shouted Susie, rushing to the front door. 'In a police car, too. The police must have been quick off the mark, Binkie.'

'Yes. But I was pretty scared when we went to the police station, and told them about the Seven and that horrid Alsatian dog guarding them,' said Binkie. 'I'm sure that first policeman we saw didn't believe us.'

'Jack! Did the police rescue you?' shouted Susie, and to Jack's great surprise, she rushed to him and gave him a bear-hug. 'I *was* so worried!' she said. 'What happened?'

Jack told her how the police car and van had come, and how the wonderful dog-handler and his charges had tamed the ferocious Nabber. 'I *wish* I'd seen him!' said Binkie. 'You Secret Seven do have marvellous times together.'

'Well – this adventure was pretty scary some-times,' said Jack. 'Honestly I don't know what we'd have done if you and Binkie hadn't come along – snoopers though you are! By the way, Susie, how *did* you know where we'd gone? *Did* you look in my notebook? I expect I made a note there about where we were going. You *shouldn't* read people's private writing.'

'I know,' said Susie. 'But I get so curious when I'm sure that you and the others have something exciting on hand – and when I found your notebook on the floor, well – I just couldn't help myself. I picked it up and read it and then I telephoned Binkie, and we took out our bikes to follow you. Just as well we did!'

'Well – it was, as it happened,' said Jack. 'But it was a *snoopy* thing to do, Susie. Only girls do that sort of thing.'

'Aha! Does Janet snoop then? And Barbara and Pam?' cried Binkie.

'No. Of course not,' said Jack, and hurriedly changed the subject. 'Anyway, it was jolly good of you and Susie to help us when we were in such a fix. I was scared stiff of that Alsatian. I think his name's a very good one, don't you? Nabber! I'm glad he didn't nab *me*!'

The next morning was rather exciting. The police saw all the Secret Seven, and listened to their story of the finding of the hidden medals in the tree. 'But what we'd *really* like to know,' said one of the police officers, 'is where on earth the *medals* are! They weren't in the pockets of either of the thieves, and they seemed as puzzled as we were to know where they had disappeared to. Tom Smith produced the medal case out of his pocket – but when he opened it, no medals were there! It was empty! We searched both men, but found nothing.'

'Strange,' said Peter, solemnly, and Janet nodded.

'Very curious,' said Barbara and Pam, trying not to giggle.

'*Most* extraordinary!' said George and Jack.

'It would be interesting to know where the medals *are*,' said Colin, frowning.

The others grinned behind his back, marvelling that Colin could keep such a straight face. They all knew that he had the glittering medals in his pocket, carefully wrapped in tissue paper that he had taken from his mother's cupboard. Peter had handed them to him just an hour ago, and had told him that he, and he alone, must give them to the old General, as soon as he had a chance.

Colin had been a little uneasy when Peter handed him the medals. 'You're SURE that it doesn't matter *me* handing them back to the General, instead of the police taking them to him?' he said, anxiously. 'They won't be angry with me, will they? It's only because we don't want him to have to hand out a large reward that he can't possibly afford.'

'Look – you go and give them to him as soon as you get a chance,' Peter said. 'I know we *all* had a share in discovering them, Colin – but it was *you* who promised to bring them back.'

And now the time had come to take the medals to the old General. Colin felt decidedly nervous. How shall I explain it all? he thought. How can I tell him all about Tom Smith and Wily and Nabber? I shall get into a terrible muddle, and so will he. I think I'll just push them into his hand.

He didn't go over the garden wall this time, but knocked politely at the front door. Emma opened it. 'Why, it's you, Colin,' she said. 'Come away in. The police are here, but they'll be gone in a minute.'

'The police? Oh, then I'll come another time,' began Colin, in fright, but Emma hustled him along the passage and into the sitting-room.

The old General was there, and so were the police officers who had driven the police cars the night before.

'The boy from next door to see you,' said Emma, pushing Colin before her. General Branksome beamed at Colin.

'Good morning, Colin. I've something to tell you! The police have brought me back the case my medals were in, and they are rather hopeful of getting back the medals too. What do you think of that?'

'We have no idea at present where the medals are,' said one police officer, hurriedly. He turned to

Colin. 'Perhaps you can make the gentleman understand that we really haven't much hope,' he said.
'We just thought he'd like the case back, medals or
no medals.'

'Colin here said *he'd* bring me back my medals,'
said the General, beaming round. 'And I believe him.
He's that sort of boy – does what he says he will do.
Fine type of lad. Lives next door to me.'

'May I have the medal case, please?' asked Colin,
solemnly, and the General picked up the empty
box and gave it to him. Colin opened it. Then he
put his hand in his pocket, and took out the little
bundle of medals wrapped carefully in soft tissue
paper. He unwrapped them one by one and put
them gently back into their places in the leather
case.

The two policemen couldn't believe their eyes!
They watched Colin, too amazed to speak. The
medals! Shining gold medals! Perhaps they were
dreaming?

The General watched too, a beaming smile on his wrinkled old face. 'Ha, what did I tell you?' he said to the two surprised men. 'I told you this boy said he'd get them back – I knew he'd keep his word. He's that kind of boy. HE shall have the reward! FIVE HUNDRED POUNDS!'

'No, thank you,' said Colin, hurriedly. 'No, THANK YOU VERY MUCH. We don't want the reward. That's why I was told to bring them back to you myself – so that you wouldn't have to pay out such a large sum of money. We – er – we enjoyed getting them back very much indeed.'

The two police officers stared at Colin in silence. They had been pleased at least to bring back the empty medal case – but this boy had brought back the medals themselves!

'Er – we'll have to ask you a few questions, boy,' said one of the officers. 'The first thing is – where did you and your friends get these? We've hunted all over the place for them.'

'They were in a hole in a tree,' said Colin, beginning to enjoy himself.

'Indeed – and did *you* put them there by any chance?' asked the officer.

'Oh! no. Wily put them there,' said Colin, solemnly. 'He has such small hands, sir.'

The General had now put all his medals back into the case, and had hung it up in its usual place over the mantelpiece. He went to the door and shouted, looking ten years younger.

'EMMA! I have company! Bring something to eat and drink. EMMA, MY MEDALS ARE BACK!'

The two police officers couldn't stay to chat and eat and drink with the old man, so they said goodbye, patted Colin on the back, and went, looking rather puzzled.

'Pity that boy didn't come and tell *us*,' said the first officer.

'No. No, I think it was right that *he* should take them back to the General,' said the second officer. 'It does seem that *he* promised to find them for him.'

'Odd, that,' said the first officer. 'He can't possibly have known where they were.'

'Well – if people very, very much want to do something for somebody else, somehow they find a way,' said the second officer. 'Haven't you ever noticed that?'

The old General was as happy as a boy all that day, and how he enjoyed hearing the whole story from Colin! He told Emma about 'that boy, Colin' a score of times. 'If only I could think of something to give him – and something for his friends too!' he said. 'You see, Emma, they won't take the reward. There are seven of them – and two girls helped besides, called Binkie and Susie – and I believe there's a dog called Run-Along, or something like that.'

'Oh, you mean Scamper!' said Emma. 'Now look, General, what do you yourself feel most proud of, what do you most love looking at and wearing?'

'Well, my medals, of course,' said the General.

'Right. Then why don't you give those children medals too – just little ones – with their names on one side – and with "FOR BRAVERY" the other side. Because, from all I've heard, they *were* brave!'

'Emma, you *do* think of fine ideas,' said the General, pleased. 'Of course – just the thing! Medals! And I'll ask if I can go to their next meeting and pin them all on. Ha – what a fine time we shall have!'

So next week there is to be an extra special meeting down in the shed, with the General presiding, and pinning on ten medals – yes, Binkie and Susie are to have one each too. Peter says that is only fair.

Ten, did I say? Let me see – seven for the Secret Seven, one each for Binkie and Susie. That's nine.

'Wuff-wuff-wuff!' Oh, of *course*, Scamper, the tenth one is for *you*. You were in the adventure, too. How proud you will be when you race about with a medal swinging from the front of your collar! Congratulations to you and all the Secret Seven – and may you have many more adventures!

Read on for more stories
and fun facts about
THE SECRET SEVEN!

ABOUT THE SECRET SEVEN

The Secret Seven Society consists of Peter, his sister Janet, and their friends Jack, Colin, George, Pam and Barbara. Peter and Janet's golden spaniel Scamper also attends meetings, which are held in a shed with S.S. on the door. Admission is by password only and badges must be worn. Peter, as head of the society, makes sure that everyone follows the rules!

The Seven puzzle over strange goings-on in their local community, aiming to solve mysteries and put things right. Their work often involves hiding and keeping watch, hunting for clues, shadowing suspicious characters and questioning people. Burglaries, stolen animals and missing children feature in various stories – as do fireworks, a tree-house, a telescope and Susie's toy aeroplane.

The first of the fifteen Secret Seven books was published in 1949, with the final title appearing in 1963. However, Peter and Janet had appeared in an earlier book called *At Seaside Cottage* (1947) and the story of the formation of the society had been told in the short story Secret of the Old Mill (1948.) There are five other Secret Seven short stories, which are gathered together in *The Secret Seven Short Story Collection*.

Enid Blyton rewrote the Secret Seven stories so they could be adapted into cartoons. These were published in the *Mickey Mouse Weekly* in 1951. They were illustrated by George Brook, who was one of the original illustrators of the series.

A Secret Seven card game was launched in 1955 and in 1954, four Secret Seven jigsaw puzzles appeared from Bestime. Whitman released four new jigsaw puzzles in 1975. In the 1970s, Evelyne Lallemand wrote a 12-book series of Secret Seven continuation books in French, nine of which were translated into English by Anthea Bell between 1983 and 1987, but they are long out of print. Between 1978 and 1984, the Secret Seven could be found in annuals.

LET'S HAVE A CLUB OF OUR OWN – PART FIVE

Now that all the rules and regulations are in place, it's time to have some fun! Have you enjoyed the journey so far? The first four parts are printed in the previous four Secret Seven mysteries.

'Let's do bird-watching down at the lake, for one thing,' suggested Eric promptly.

Dick opened his mouth to say No, that was too dull – and then stayed silent. He remembered that Eric was lame, and couldn't go tree-climbing, or on long hikes – one of the Club's interests, at least, should be something *he* could do.

'A good idea, Eric,' said Mark, at once. 'We are all interested in birds and belong to the school's nature-club. We can do regular bird-watching, and write up what we see and hear for the School Nature Magazine

– and we'll sign our article "The Sturdy Six!" Any other suggestions?'

'Could we collect used postage stamps and tinfoil, and take them to the hospital?' asked Katie. 'They sell them and buy toys for the children there. I know that Mollie and I already do this, but we'd get on much faster with our collections if we could *all* bring some to each meeting.'

'Agreed!' cried everyone, and Mark looked at Katie. 'You will be put in charge of that,' he said to her. 'Provide a bag for the silver paper or tinfoil, please, and a tin for the used stamps, and leave them here. We will bring what we have, each time there is a meeting – and you and Katie will be responsible for taking the tin and the bag, when full, to the Secretary at the hospital.'

'Yes, Mark,' said both girls together. Ha – *now* they would soon get a good collection!

'And what about doing a play or something, and charging for the tickets?' said James. 'You know the

Head said the other day at Prayers that the school really must raise money to buy more books for the Class Libraries – and why shouldn't the Sturdy Six show what can be done?'

Everyone agreed in delight. 'Yes! We'll do a show! We'll ask the Head if we can!' said Dick. 'My word – we're going to be busy. But wouldn't it be better to do that at Christmas time?'

They discussed the matter thoroughly, and Mark looked at his Club members with approval. Who would have thought that at the second meeting the club would be going so strong – and that ideas would be pouring out, and everyone would be so eager and interested? He felt very pleased with the Sturdy Six!

He stopped the discussion at last, after having listened to everyone's suggestions.

'As far as I can gather, you are most of you in favour of a Christmas show,' he said. 'And it would certainly be something to do in the dark evenings next term.

We'll put it to the vote. Hands up those who are in favour of doing the play now.'

Not a hand went up! 'Well, hands up for doing the play at Christmas,' said Mark, grinning, and every hand shot up, of course! 'That's decided, then,' said Mark. 'But couldn't we do something this summer, too – have a garden sale, or something?'

'Oh, *yes!*' said Katie and Mollie together. 'A *jumble* sale would be wonderful,' added Mollie. 'Jumble sells like anything, and it's so easy to go round and ask people if they want to throw away anything, and if so, to give it to us instead, as we want to hold a sale in aid of – in aid of . . . well, what *shall* it be in aid of, because the *play* will be to get money for books for the Class Libraries. We shan't need any more money for that!'

'Just this,' said James and lightly touched his two shoulders, one with each hand.

'Ideas, please,' said Mark, at once, and ideas came, of course!

'For the Sunshine Homes for Blind Children! For helping animals! For children in hospital! For buying a radio set for that poor blind old Mr. Sykes who sits at his window alone all day! For – for – for . . .'

'Enough,' said Mark, putting up his hand. 'You are full of good ideas! I don't see why we can't adopt *all* your ideas, and, when we've had the sale, and counted up the money we get, we could divide it between the things suggested.'

'Yes! And if we raise any money on our own, that could go towards our ideas too,' said Katie. 'For instance, my father has promised me a shilling a week for keeping his bicycle clean. I'd willingly put that towards something.'

'And I can take old Mrs. Lucy's two dogs out for a walk in the evenings, and earn *two* shillings a week,' said Eric. 'I can't walk very fast – but the dogs are old and fat and like ambling along.'

'I can earn a shilling or two by doing the washing-up!' said Mollie.

'And I can earn *ten* shillings if I want to, by washing my uncle's car twice a week,' said Dick proudly.

In fact, everyone knew how they could earn little or much, and they all became very excited in talking about it. Mark had to clap his hands loudly to get silence. 'I shall really have to borrow my Dad's hammer,' he said grinning, 'and bang it on the floor for silence! This Club is about the liveliest in the country, I should think!'

Our story has one more part to unfold. Don't miss the conclusion in Fun for the Secret Seven.

THE LIFE AND TIMES OF ENID BLYTON

1960S

January 30, 1960 Enid's first appearance in *Princess* with 'Five at Finniston Farm'.

October, 1961 Hamlyn publish *The Big Enid Blyton Book*, the only book in which Enid broke her golden rule of never accepting a 'publisher's advance'.

1962 Armada Books is launched, so that children can buy their own paperback books. Enid Blyton is seen as key to the success of the launch.

Noddy book sales reach 26 million copies.

Enid sells Manor Farm at Stourton Caundle, Dorset.

May 25, 1963   Enid's first appearance in *School Friend* – with 'Bravo Secret Seven'.

July   The last book in each of the **Famous Five** and **Secret Seven** series are published.

February, 1964   *Noddy and the Aeroplane* – the last book in the Noddy Library series.

Film *Five Have A Mystery To Solve* released by Rayant

Pictures Ltd for the Children's Film Foundation.

May, 1965   *Mixed Bag* published – a song book for which her nephew, Carey Blyton writes the music.

August   *The Man Who Stopped to Help* and *The Boy Who Came Back* published – the last full-length books to be written by Enid.

September 15, 1967 Enid's husband, Kenneth, dies. She writes in her diary: 'My darling Kenneth died. I loved him so much. I feel lost and unhappy'.

November 28, 1968 Enid Blyton dies peacefully in her sleep in a nursing home in Hampstead, London

For the rest of Enid's life, look in the back of the previous six Secret Seven titles ...

WHY I WRITE SO MANY BOOKS

This is an extract from The Story of My Life, *Enid Blyton's autobiography, published in 1952. She loved hearing from her readers, and this book was written for them.*

One thing that always puzzles the grown-ups but, as far as I know, has never puzzled you children, is why I write so many books – and so many different kinds.

Now, most authors like one age of children best – perhaps six years old, or ten, or thirteen. So they write for their favourite age, and that age only. Let us say that an author prefers the age of six. Very well – the child arrives at six years old, that author's books are given to him, and he reads them and loves them. When you were small you probably read some of Beatrix Potter's enchanting animal books – but when you grew a little older, and were no longer six years old, you didn't read her books any more. There were no more of them to read, because she only wrote for very young children.

Other authors prefer to write for much older children. They have no interest in the younger ones, and would probably write boring books for them if they went outside the age-range they have chosen – which is, say, teenage. But you children then have to wait for years before you are of the age to read that author.

Now, I like every single age of child there is. I like babies, of course, and toddlers – but when the child is between two and three years old I think it is time he had stories told to him. I did so love stories when I was little and I never had enough of them. I love writing stories for the tinies, so I begin with them at about three years old – though sometimes parents tell me that their two-year-olds love to listen to simple stories.

But I don't want to stop at three-year-olds! I like you just as much when you are five and six – and just as much when you are nine and ten, and in your teens. In fact, as I said, I like every single age of child there is. I want to know you from the very beginning, and go with you all through your childhood till you are old enough to read adult books. I don't want you to be friends with me at one age only, I want to keep in touch with you all through your childhood days.

And so I write for you from the time you first begin to like stories, right up to the day when you turn to adult books.

My mind has always been a restless, ever-working one. I want to try everything. I wanted to write nature books and I wanted to write adventure stories. I felt that I must write fairy-tales, and I must also write annuals, because you love them so much. I couldn't help writing farm stories, because I love farm life, and it was impossible not to write school stories, especially when my own children went to school.

Then I felt that I must write circus stories. I loved the circus so much when I was a child. I do still, of course. I went behind the scenes once and I have never forgotten it. I was about nine years old then, and after that a great many of the 'night-thoughts' that came to me were about the circus. Before long my imagination had created a whole circus – and so naturally, when I grew up and wanted to write, one of the things I found it easy to do was to write books about circuses.

I wanted to write 'home stories' too – books about families and how they get on together – like *House-at-the-Corner* and *Those Dreadful Children*. I felt that I must try my hand at detective stories, where the children themselves are detectives – and so the Mystery series began, with Fatty, Larry, Pip, Bets and Mr Goon in it.

Oddly enough, you liked them all. If I happened to write two books about the same characters, in came floods of letters, saying that it *must* be a series, when was the third one coming out? How you do love books about the same characters, don't you? I do myself.

There was no end to the kinds of books I wanted to write, which I knew you needed or would love to have. What did it matter if it was hard work, I loved every minute!

HOW WELL DO YOU REMEMBER
LOOK OUT, SECRET SEVEN?

Here are questions to test your memory. The answers are printed on the next page, but they're upside down. No cheating!

1. What present does Auntie Lou give Janet and Peter?

2. How does Susie sneak into the Secret Seven's meeting?

3. What has been stolen from General Branksome?

4. Where do the Secret Seven agree to keep an eye on birds' nests?

5. What excuse does Colin come up with to visit the General?

6. How much money does the General offer as a reward for the return of his medals?

7. What kind of bird's nest are the boys robbing when George and Barbara find them?

8. What is the name of the man the Secret Seven share their picnic with?

9. What kind of animal disturbs Colin and George while they are hiding?

10. What is the name of the thieves' Alsatian?

11. Who finds the Secret Seven in the forest and goes for help?

12. What does the General give the Seven as a reward?

1. A big tin of chocolate biscuits. 2. She dresses up as Jack. 3. His medals. 4. Bramley Woods. 5. He pretends to lose his ball over the wall. 6. Five hundred pounds. 7. A blackbird's. 8. Tom Smith. 9. A squirrel. 10. Nabber. 11. Susie and Binkie. 12. Medals of their own!

START YOUR
SECRET SEVEN CLUB

In each of the Tony Ross editions of The Secret Seven is a Club Token (see below). Collect any five tokens and you'll get a brilliant Secret Seven club pack – perfect for you and your friends to start your very own secret club!

GET THE SECRET SEVEN CLUB PACK:

7 club pencils

7 club bookmarks

1 club poster

7 club badges

Simply fill in the form below, send it in with your five tokens, and we'll send you the club pack!

Send to:

Secret Seven Club, Hachette Children's Books, Marketing Department, 338 Euston Road, London NW1 3BH

Closing date: 31st December 2013

TERMS AND CONDITIONS:

(1) Open to UK and Republic of Ireland residents only (2) You must provide the email address of a parent or guardian for your entry to be valid (3) Photocopied tokens are not accepted (4) The form must be completed fully for your entry to be valid (5) Club packs are distributed on a first come, first served basis while stocks last (6) No part of the offer is exchangeable for cash or any other offer (7) Please allow 28 days for delivery (8) Your details will only be used for the purposes of fulfilling this offer and, if you choose [see tick box below], to send email newsletters about Enid Blyton and other great Hachette Children's books, and will never be shared with any third party.

Please complete using capital letters (UK Residents Only)

FIRST NAME:

SURNAME:

DATE OF BIRTH: DD | MM | YYYY

ADDRESS LINE 1:

ADDRESS LINE 2:

ADDRESS LINE 3:

POSTCODE:

PARENT OR GUARDIAN'S EMAIL ADDRESS:

☐ I'd like to receive a regular Enid Blyton email newsletter and information about other great Hachette Children's books (I can unsubscribe at any time).

1 SECRET SEVEN CLUB TOKEN

www.thesecretseven.co.uk

THE SECRET SEVEN ONLINE

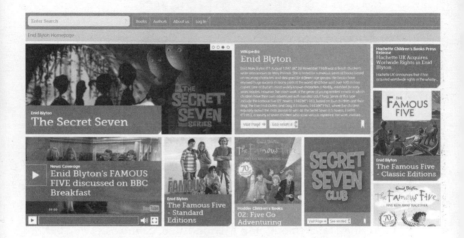

ON THE WEBSITE, YOU CAN:-

- Download and make your very own **SECRET SEVEN** door hanger

- Get tips on how to set up your own **SECRET SEVEN** club

- Find **SECRET SEVEN** snack recipes for your own club meetings

- Take the **SECRET SEVEN** quiz to see how much you really know!

- Sign up to get news of brilliant competitions and more great books

AND MUCH MORE!

GO TO ... **WWW.THESECRETSEVEN.CO.UK** AND JOIN IN!